"Sasha Lindsey. Glad to finally meet you, Mr. Price."

Sasha's grip was firm, strong, and didn't last nearly long enough. *Eyes up, Nic. Fuck!*

"Call me Nic." As much as he enjoyed the sound of Sasha calling him "Mister," he didn't relish being called by his father's name. He'd love to sort the kids out about proper treatment of his home in his absence, but he needed to deal with the manny first. Maybe without the audience, though.

As he led the way to the foyer, Nic clenched his jaw. He didn't have time or energy to fix things with the kids yet, not with the company struggling, his parents breathing down his neck, and all his late hours. A good start would be getting rid of this manny, who obviously couldn't maintain discipline with them.

Problem was, now that he'd seen the manny, he wasn't sure his libido was ready to get rid of the golden-haired Adonis.

WELCOME TO

Dear Reader,

Love is the dream. It dazzles us, makes us stronger, and brings us to our knees. Dreamspun Desires tell stories of love featuring your favorite heartwarming heroes, captivating plots, and exotic locations. Stories that make your breath catch and your imagination soar.

In the pages of these wonderful love stories, readers can escape to a world where love conquers all, the tenderness of a first kiss sweeps you away, and your heart pounds at the sight of the one you love.

When you put it all together, you find romance in its truest form.

Love always finds a way.

Elizabeth North

Executive Director
Dreamspinner Press

Angela McCallister

THE CEO'S CHRISTMAS MANNY

DREAMSPUN DESIRES

PUBLISHED BY

Published by
DREAMSPINNER PRESS

5032 Capital Circle SW, Suite 2, PMB# 279,
Tallahassee, FL 32305-7886 USA
www.dreamspinnerpress.com

The CEO's Christmas Manny
© 2018 Angela McCallister.
Editorial Development by Sue Brown-Moore.

Cover Art
© 2018 Alexandria Corza.
http://www.seeingstatic.com/
Cover content is for illustrative purposes only and any person depicted
on the cover is a model.

Paperback ISBN: 978-1-64108-147-4
Digital ISBN: 978-1-64405-120-7
Library of Congress Control Number: 2018956962
Paperback published December 2018
v. 1.0

Printed in the United States of America
∞
This paper meets the requirements of
ANSI/NISO Z39.48-1992 (Permanence of Paper).

Mom of five mostly grown kids, US Navy veteran, and total book ho who reads at least two dozen romances of various subgenres each month, **ANGELA MCCALLISTER** writes paranormal, sci-fi, and contemporary romance. Spanning from CEO billionaires to space vampires, paranormal matchmakers, and tech nerds, she crafts sexy romances with riveting characters who make you laugh, cry, and curse. She's best known for her random accidental humor, her silly sea stories, her terrible memory, and her love of creepy-crawly pets and ridiculously cheesy sci-fi/horror movies. Enjoy those too? She loves to hear from readers. Find her on Facebook or Twitter to chat and exchange recs.

Web: www.angelamccallister.com

Twitter: @AngMcCallister

Facebook: www.facebook.com/AngelaMcCallisterAuthor

Pinterest: pinterest.com/AngMcCallister

For Sue Brown-Moore whose invitation opened doors.

Acknowledgments

MY life wouldn't be complete without Rachael Davish and Natalie Bilski to pull me back from the ledge (and help patch my plot holes). I wouldn't get much accomplished without your advice and encouragement, and I'm sure Lucy and Ben might have fallen short without you. Thank you so very much to Ellie C and Angela P for being such great friends and beta readers. Still can't believe all of you were willing to endure such conversations as Elf on a Shelf scenarios and theater sex.

Chapter One

Nic

NO matter how hard Nicolas stared at the projected revenue numbers in front of him, they wouldn't magically improve for this quarter. He barely listened as the special project team he'd assembled last month went over his best hope to stave off the third straight quarter of lost revenue for his family business. The weight pressing down on his chest had never been so great, but he usually performed best under such pressure. So why couldn't he focus this time?

"Mr. Price?" A little nudge and deep voice at his shoulder brought his attention to Percy, his assistant, who crouched beside his chair, trying to be unobtrusive. Impossible. Percy looked nothing like a CEO's executive assistant—more like the star of a superspy thriller featuring special warfare soldiers or mercenaries. There was no helping that because, aside from their friendship, security qualifications *were* the primary reasons he'd chosen Percy.

At the interruption, his VP had paused, so Nicolas motioned for her to continue the presentation while he stepped outside the conference room to speak to Percy. There weren't any details about the proposed Italian deal Nic hadn't already examined extensively anyway.

"Sorry, boss."

"It's okay. Not missing much in there." He waved carelessly toward the conference room door, and then his gut tightened at the sober expression on Percy's square-jawed face. The guy always looked like he'd missed a shave and spent all night awake, but now it was more a sense of his inner tension bleeding out. "What happened?"

"The school called. The truancy officer caught Benedict skipping this afternoon."

Damn. Not again. The kids would be the death of him. It'd been four years since he'd become sole guardian of his niece and nephew after their parents died in a fatal car crash. At first, he'd been understanding of their unruly behavior. They'd been quite young, Benedict only eight and Lucille slightly older at age twelve. Nic's sister, their mother, had mostly grown up in his aunt's household, leaving Nicolas feeling much like an only child, which made him ill-equipped to raise Josephine's children in her absence. His beloved sister was, no doubt, looking down on him in disgust from the afterlife.

"Perfect." Nicolas drew his hands over his face and sighed. "Have the governess—"

"Resigned this morning."

That's all Percy needed to say. The kids had gone through at least two caretakers per year since he'd taken custody of them. It had become nearly a matter of routine to contact the service for a new nanny or governess.

Nicolas presented his friend with his best pleading look. He wouldn't dream of this with any other employee, but Percy was more than just another employee to him since they'd gone to college together. Of course Percy didn't need words to interpret his meaning.

"Really?" Percy's left eyebrow arched. "Are you kidding me?"

He grasped Percy's shoulder. "Just this time. I have to get ready for Italy to finalize the purchase. This deal will drop expenditures drastically and put an end to our vanishing profits. I have to make this the priority right now."

When resignation settled on Percy's face, some of the tension released from Nic's muscles. Percy would deal with the school and watch the kids today until Nicolas returned home.

"Oh, and please contact the service for a new governess. We need someone right away. I'm leaving for Italy tomorrow."

"So soon?" Surprise widened Percy's gray eyes right before they grew reproachful. "I thought you'd wait until after Thanksgiving. Do the kids know?"

Nicolas dropped his arm to his side. "No, but they're fine. They keep to themselves and have their friends when they aren't in school or doing homework. They don't even like Thanksgiving. It won't matter."

Percy grumbled something under his breath as he headed down the hallway toward the elevators. "All right," he called over his shoulder. "I'm taking care of this."

"Thank you. You're a saint."

With an exasperated groan, Percy stopped and turned. "I can't believe I'm telling you this again, Nic, but you don't have enough balance in your life. All this?" He waved at the walls. "It's a thing that only consumes. It won't make you happy. Or anyone else around you, for that matter."

Nicolas tried not to bristle at his friend's old argument. "I only need to get the numbers up for a few quarters. It takes time and attention, and it does make me happy to make money and be successful. It gets my parents off my back, and that couldn't make me happier."

"Well, it's always going to need time and attention. That's what employees are for. Lean on them once in a while so you can put that money you earn to good use. You know, have some fun or something. Get a hobby. Christ, Nic, you're missing Thanksgiving at home, and it's almost Christmas. *Spend time with your niece and nephew.*"

Percy didn't wait for a response but jogged over to catch the elevator while it was open. The bastard didn't hesitate to send Nic a smug smile that said it was a pleasure to get in the last word.

Nicolas waited for the doors to close before he headed back to finish the meeting. It was the longest half hour of his life and shed no new inspiration on how to fix this fiscal year's first quarter revenue before the end of December. Even if things went as Nic planned, it would take time to see the impact of increased sales and lowered costs.

He'd barely made it back to his office and poured himself a glass of chilled water with lemon and mint before his secretary buzzed him.

"Summer, I thought I told you to hold my calls."

"Sorry, sir. It's your father." Summer's voice was soft and genuinely apologetic, so it was hard to be upset with her. Also, his father wasn't the kind of man to take a brush-off well. Nicolas Leighton Price II wasn't one to take anything but strict obedience well.

"It's all right. Put him through."

Nic pulled at his neatly tailored charcoal suit jacket and straightened his tie until he noticed what he was doing. It was only a damned phone call. He sipped his water and cleared his throat before hitting the button to take the line.

"Good afternoon, Father."

"Son." A series of loud thwacking sounds in the background told Nicolas his father was at the driving range. "Your mother and I have been talking about the health of Leighton Price."

Nausea speared its claws into Nic's stomach. He'd been expecting something like this, a lecture about how he'd let the company slip, but he'd hoped it would wait at least one more quarter.

"Well, it's good you brought it up. With the nationwide recession, business has been a little slow to pick up, but we already have a solid plan of action to get the numbers up by next quarter." Nicolas hoped to cut his father off at the pass and get this conversation postponed until he could get his plans more decisively confirmed.

"It's late in the game for that. A solid plan should have been acted on in the first quarter the revenue dropped. Wouldn't you agree?"

It wasn't the words his father used but the thick derision they soaked in that sank ice into Nic's blood. His father didn't care why profits had declined over the last few quarters. He didn't care that businesses in the

US across the board were experiencing such losses. He only cared that Nicolas was a disappointment, a failure. He wanted to grind in the knowledge that he found Nicolas lacking, and he wanted to make Nicolas admit to being inadequate.

"I would agree we gained new clients that quarter at a record rate and cut expenditures by over 20 percent. We made changes that ensured we'd have a profit that quarter instead of a deficit."

His father voiced a sound close to a growl, something Nicolas had rarely heard since he was a child. "I don't want to hear excuses. We've waited long enough, and as the majority shareholders, your mother and I have decided to make some changes of our own."

Nicolas gripped his armrest hard enough to crease the leather. "What changes?"

"We're replacing you as the CEO of Leighton Price if you don't increase revenue by the end of the quarter. As I have no intention of coming out of retirement to run the company again, you need to have a plan for an heir. Benedict had better be on track to take over when he's old enough, or you need to produce your own suitable heir. If this isn't done, we're considering going public with the company."

"Father, it's going to take more than one quar—"

"I didn't call to ask your opinion or have a discussion. This is what the family has decided. Your mother and I can't keep letting you slack off, and frankly, we're tired of being disappointed in you. I think you've let us down long enough. It's time to be a man, make good decisions, and get the company back on track. If you don't, we're replacing you."

"Father."

Nicolas didn't bother saying more. The phone line was already dead before he'd said a word. He dropped his forehead onto his desk, struggling to draw each breath, but even the air felt oppressive. This company was everything, his life. He had nothing else. He'd worked so hard and invested endless hours to make it the best it could be—nights, holidays, weekends, all spent at the altar of his family legacy.

Nicolas sat back in his seat and shook his head. Fuck this. He'd worked too hard for everything to be handed over to some interloper. He still had the Italian deal, so he'd fly to Italy in the morning, purchase the Italian leather company there, and pick up a few new clients before the holidays. This plan would be enough to lower costs, increase revenue, and give him just enough profit to beat last quarter's stats and save his seat as CEO.

Dammit, it had to be enough. He was nothing without this company.

Chapter Two

Sasha

SASHA took a last look around the middle-school classroom that had been his domain for the past year. Of all the jobs he'd bounced around to and from, this was the toughest to leave. Damn, he missed these kids already, and he hadn't even walked out the door yet with his pitiful box of personal belongings. If ever he was the kind of guy to cry, now would be the time, but as always, he wouldn't allow it. He hadn't allowed it when his parents had routinely abandoned him as a child. He hadn't allowed it even when he'd caught his boyfriend, Drew, getting it on with another man in their shared apartment.

In the latter case, though, maybe it was his anger toward Drew that kept his sharpest emotions at bay. If Drew weren't a tenured teacher at the middle school, Sasha could have happily fought to keep his job here. But Drew and his boy toy were in the same math department as Sasha. It also didn't help that their apartment was in Drew's name, even though Sasha paid most of the rent. This all left him without a job, without a home, and utterly alone. Always alone in the end. And this time right before the holidays.

Considering his admittedly abundant list of friends, none of them were the kind to turn to in times of trouble. They were the ones to call to party or go drinking with. Wouldn't getting drunk be peachy? In his drunken stupor, he'd end up trying to go to a home he no longer had. Nope. His new to-do list involved cramming what few possessions he owned into his beloved truck, heading for a hotel, and hoping it didn't rain. The way his life was going, there'd probably be a downpour before he'd gone ten miles.

As he reached for his box of belongings, his phone rang. Ah, what the hell. There wouldn't be a class coming in until next period, and he didn't work here anymore. He pulled it from his pocket and glanced at it, a Seattle number. He answered before it went to voicemail.

"Hello. I'm calling for Ms. Sasha Lindsey."

Sasha chuckled. It never got old how everyone assumed he was a female. "That's Mr. Sasha Lindsey, and you've got him."

There was an awkward pause. "Oh, uh, I'm so sorry. I called to schedule your interview for the nanny position you applied for. Was there a mistake? Perhaps you didn't apply for the job?"

More like she was hoping he hadn't applied for the job. He wasn't about to let her off the hook, and he had nowhere else to be anyway. May as well make the drive from California to Washington to have the interview. Seattle was as good a place as any to make a fresh start.

"I did apply, and I'd love to interview in person. You'll find I'm highly qualified and have exceptional references. As I'm a school teacher, you'll also find I pass rigorous background checks."

The woman stuttered a few times, but eventually they worked out a time and date that would allow him to make the drive and have time to find a hotel before he had to be there. After he hung up, he grabbed his box and headed out to his truck. After sliding behind the wheel, he pulled his phone out again. To be honest, he didn't remember which job he'd blindly agreed to interview for. Not that it mattered. He'd sent out about thirty applications trying to get anywhere but here, where his guts wanted to spill on the pavement to match the pain in his chest.

Blowing out a hard breath, he tried to let the negativity go while he looked up the job in his email. Ah, this was a good one, though it wasn't exactly in Seattle like he'd assumed. He'd be working in Vashon, an island in the Puget Sound across from Seattle and accessible by ferry. The posting was for a live-in nanny with room and board provided, a driver, and a discretionary fund on top of a salary.

Living on an island would be different, but otherwise, the job was perfect. He'd have a place to live and food to eat so he wouldn't have to worry about stretching his money or living in his truck until his first payday. Yes, his beast of a Silverado was his life, the only extravagant thing he'd allowed himself, but he wasn't ready to make it his home address.

If only he hadn't paid the rent on Drew's apartment this month already. Come to think of it, he'd always been the one to pay for Drew, and even their friends, when they went out. While Drew had been saving his money. Or spending it on his side guy. Fuck.

A knock on his window startled him from his thoughts. He looked up from his phone and rolled the window down when he saw one of his students—former students.

"Mr. Lindsey? Are you really leaving?"

"Yeah. I'm sorry, Mark. I wish I'd had enough time to say goodbye to all my classes."

The kid's shoulders slumped. "There's no way they could replace you."

Sasha gave him a broad smile, trying to keep his real feelings from showing. "Oh, don't worry. I'm sure the new teacher will know his stuff."

"Maybe," the kid said, "but he won't make it fun. I don't think anyone can make math fun like you do."

"You don't know that. Even if he's not fun, remember all those websites I gave you if you get to stuff you don't understand. They'll make it easier for you. They make games out of it. You can make anything fun if you get creative and put your mind to it."

Mark stared at the ground as he spoke. "You never treated us like we didn't matter."

"Because you do matter. You all do. Look, you're fourteen. Only a few more years and you'll be a young adult. If people want to treat you like a little kid, it's their problem. It's not because you aren't capable of being more mature, and it doesn't mean you have to act the way they treat you."

"We'll miss you." Mark did look up then, and it drove the pain through Sasha's practiced numbness. His smile fell away.

"I'll miss all of you too. Very much. I'm honored to have met you, Mark."

The conversation echoed in his head on repeat as Sasha packed his belongings that afternoon. So many times, he'd had to leave jobs like this over failed relationships. He should have learned not to make attachments at work that would compromise his job. This was a dose of the consequences, and he wasn't throwing this lesson away.

If he got this job in Vashon, it wasn't only for financial security and a place to live. It was a chance to make a difference in kids' lives, the entire reason he'd become a teacher. He'd be taking care of a twelve-year-old boy and a sixteen-year-old girl, and for once, he had every intention of staying until they didn't need him anymore.

Should be a piece of cake. The parents were probably a middle-aged married couple who worked high-powered jobs somewhere that kept them away from home a lot. Maybe they'd be surprised to find he was male, but it was an ideal position. At least there was no chance the dad would find Sasha attractive and start banging the nanny.

Chapter Three

Nic

THE rich leather of his town car was trying its damnedest to drag Nic into a nap on his long ride home from the airport. Instead of succumbing to fatigue, he kept his laptop open and finished the last few memos needing attention before he could finally call it a night. His trip had been a resounding success. Two weeks of hell and hard work in Italy trying to ensure all the paperwork was complete before he left, but now, they owned a direct supply of handcrafted Italian leather, considerably cutting costs at Leighton Price. Next on the agenda, he needed to acquire a few more clients or significantly increase existing contracts.

As the car left the ferry, he clicked his laptop shut. He probably should have taken the helicopter instead of opting for the car ride. It didn't escape him that his reluctance to meet the new nanny and deal with the kids might've had something to do with his choice to delay his arrival. At least Sasha Lindsey seemed to be well-qualified, with CPR certification, a math degree, and teaching experience. After coming straight from a middle school, she had to have experience with troublesome children.

Thankfully, Percy had dealt with choosing the final candidates from the few applicants he'd found through the service, Sasha being the best one by far. At least Percy wouldn't be at the mansion when he arrived. The condemnation had practically dripped from every communiqué from Percy since Nic had left for Italy. The man was not happy Nicolas had missed Thanksgiving, though Nic couldn't figure out why his friend made such a big deal about it. No one else would miss Nic being there, most certainly not Lucy and Ben.

The car finally turned and traveled along the smooth, stone-paved drive, passing under an enclosed walkway connecting Nic's waterfront Vashon mansion to the high, rounded viewpoint tower on the north side of the driveway. After stopping right in front of the wide double doors, he didn't bother waiting for the driver before he exited the vehicle, but then, he immediately froze at the sight of his classic, slate-blue manor trimmed with white.

Usually classic. Now garish. Snaking lights in primary colors framed the abundant windows, and two enormous wreaths dwarfed the entrance, one on each door. There were so many strands of Christmas lights, it was probably causing a brownout somewhere on the island. Ridiculous. No way Percy was responsible for this wasteful display. His friend knew better than to flaunt frivolous holiday crap anywhere near him.

He'd barely taken another two steps when a glance toward the east lawn facing the waterfront froze him in place again. Huge *things* littered the manicured lawn, massive, blown-up, lit-up figures and towering candy canes taller than Nicolas. A larger-than-life Rudolph leaned over precariously and appeared to give Santa one hell of a good morning. Great. How long had these tacky monstrosities been out for the neighbors to witness?

Leaving his driver to collect his baggage, Nicolas jogged up the few steps to the door, gave one of the heavy wreaths a withering glare, and stepped through.

"Kids," he called from the foyer. "Ben. Lucy."

No one answered, but a murmur of excited voices rang out nearby. Several long steps and a right turn brought him across the foyer and into a wide-open den with floor-to-ceiling views of the water. Or what would be the view if someone hadn't puked Christmas all over his lawn.

And put a six-foot-tall tree in the center of the curved bay of windows. The sharp tang of pine permeated the room, and brittle needles littered a path to where the tree tilted pitifully to the right. No, it wasn't tilted in the stand but rather bent along the spindly trunk. Several small gaps between clumps of tree limbs resembled Ben's hair after he'd used clippers on himself a few years back.

Nic drew his focus off the eyesore in his den to the kids huddled around the coffee table in front of the sofa. Lucy squinted in concentration as she speared a piece of popcorn with a needle, her long curly blond hair trying to escape the clip restraining it at her nape. Beside her, Ben popped a few pieces of popcorn into his mouth, losing several onto the carpet, before attempting to add a piece to his short thread of homemade garland.

What the fuck? The den was trashed. It would take more than a good Hoover to suck the dried bits of tree from the carpet, and somehow, the popcorn had ended up everywhere, not only around the table where the kids worked. Nic's blood pressure shot up to dangerous levels, and his fists clenched as he fought the urge to blow up. This was the last thing he needed right now. On Sunday, his parents would be over for brunch, giving Nic only one day to get the mansion to rights before they arrived.

Another burst of laughter from the kids galvanized him, driving his feet forward until he stood over them. This situation was far from funny. Lucy and Ben should have been studying and working on homework instead of screwing around with garish Christmas decorations. The two kids noticed him finally, their laughter dying like a switch flipped somewhere. Lucy jumped to her feet, rubbing her hands down the sides of her faded jeans.

"H-Hi, Uncle Nic. Did you have a good trip?"

Not in any mood for small talk, Nic ignored her question. "What the hell is all this?" He gestured broadly around the den. "Where's Ms. Lindsey? Hasn't she been watching you two?"

Ben tucked his knees toward his chest and continued threading his popcorn without even a glance at Nic, his lips forming a tight line. However, Lucy narrowed her eyes and gave him a smirk in response.

"I'm not in the mood for games. Where is she, Lucy?"

She cleared her throat and looked over Nic's shoulder. "*Ms. Lindsey* just walked in."

Bracing himself to get rid of yet another caretaker, Nic drew a deep breath and turned. Immediately, the breath whooshed out of his lungs. A sudden gut punch couldn't have taken him more by surprise than the man standing in front of him, holding a tray with three steaming beverage mugs.

"Hi, Sasha. What took you so long?" Lucy said from behind Nic in her chirpy, fake-cheery voice. The man didn't seem to hear her at first, his bright cobalt eyes surveying Nic from top to bottom. Barefoot, his dirty blond hair deliciously tousled, and wearing somewhat loose jeans and a rumpled blue T-shirt that matched his eyes, the man—Sasha—appeared freshly rolled out from a nap.

A jolt of interest spread heat through Nic's body, centered right at his groin. If Nic had an ideal dream man, this was him—slightly shorter than Nic with broad shoulders tapered to a trim waist, an athletic build without too much bulk, and thick, iron-hard thighs perfect for wrapping securely around a man's hips.

"It's not from a mix, Lucy. Best things in life are worth waiting for." The rich, deep voice had a slight rasp to it that only added to the "just awoken" image in Nic's head, sending a lick of sensation dancing right along Nic's spine.

Despite his answer having been directed at Lucy, Sasha's eyes never strayed from Nic. After only a moment's hesitation, he continued toward Nic and leaned down beside him to place the tray on the coffee table.

As he stood, he offered his hand. "Sasha Lindsey. Glad to finally meet you, Mr. Price."

Sasha's grip was firm, strong, and didn't last nearly long enough. *Eyes up, Nic. Fuck!* Dragging his eyes away from Sasha's masculine hands, lined with sexy veins roping along his muscular arms, Nic fought the urge to drift his gaze lower to the bulge below Sasha's waistband.

"Call me Nic." As much as he enjoyed the sound of Sasha calling him "Mister," he didn't relish being called by his father's name at home on a daily basis.

When a throat cleared behind him, he glanced over his shoulder to where both kids watched him with wide eyes and raised brows. Though he'd love to sort them out about proper treatment of his home in his absence, he needed to deal with the manny first. Maybe without the audience, though.

He turned back to Sasha. "I was expecting.... Um, well."

Sasha's genuine, throaty laugh revealed sinful dimples that made Nic's breath catch in his throat.

"You were expecting a spinsterly old woman in support hose, weren't you?"

Nic couldn't help chuckling despite his frustration over the state of his house. "Something along those lines. Can you, uh, spare a few minutes to talk?" He tipped his head toward the foyer outside the den.

Sasha nodded, still grinning, and then pointed at the kids. "You two drink your cider before it gets cold."

The warmth in their answering smiles smacked into Nic's head like a two-by-four. When was the last time he'd seen them smile like that? Or smile at all? Granted he'd been gone for a couple of weeks, and he'd been too busy holding the business afloat lately to spend much time with them, but even when they were younger, the expression had been a rare occurrence. Except before, when their mother was still alive.

What would Josie think if she saw her kids now? If only there'd been someone more fitting to raise Lucy and Ben, some nurturing godparents somewhere. Because heaven knew he was fucking everything up with them. As he led the way to the foyer, Nic clenched his jaw. He didn't have time or energy to fix things with them yet, not with the company struggling, his parents breathing down his neck, and all his late hours. Fuck if he even had a clue how to deal with the kids and get them on the right track, but a good start would be getting rid of this manny, who obviously couldn't maintain discipline with them.

Problem was, now that he'd seen the manny, he wasn't sure his libido was ready to get rid of the golden-haired Adonis.

Chapter Four

Sasha

NERVES squeezed Sasha's chest at the same time desire gripped him by the balls. Nicolas Price was a real, honest-to-goodness, mature man, the kind of man who featured center stage in Sasha's fantasies, wielding authority like a second skin. He'd always had a thing for taller men, and Nic was a couple of inches taller than Sasha's six feet, lean but powerful, his muscles pulling the charcoal fabric of his suit taut as he moved. The tiny hint of premature gray at the temples of his dark head of hair sent Sasha's heartbeat fluttering.

Nic stopped and turned a few steps outside the den and then tugged his tie loose. Sasha's gaze followed his new boss's elegant, meticulously manicured fingers as they unfastened the first few buttons of his seafoam dress shirt, the color intensifying the bold emerald green of Nic's eyes. A mouthwatering glimpse of crisp, dark chest hair turned Sasha's breathing shallow while he fought to keep the arousal from showing.

"This is unacceptable, Mr. Lindsey." Nic gestured toward the den, and Sasha's stomach plummeted, effectively stomping down his runaway physical responses. It was just as well. He'd sworn not to get personally involved with anyone at work ever again, especially with an employer.

"It's Sasha, and what do you mean exactly?" Sasha's figurative hackles rose, bringing on a tension headache and a frown he couldn't help. This wasn't the first time he'd been discriminated against in the field of childcare because of his gender, but he certainly hadn't expected it from someone as educated as Nicolas Leighton Price.

"This… mess." Nic gestured again. "The crap all over the lawn, the monstrosity of a tree, and the mess in my den. I didn't expect to return to a trashed home. Did Percy have anything to do with this?"

Oh. So it wasn't about gender after all. "Trashed? Mr. Pri—Nic, do you not celebrate Christmas? I wasn't aware. The kids didn't mention anything about it, and neither did Percy."

Nic sighed, fatigue settling over his features as if he'd fought a long, hard battle only to find another one on the way back to base. Something about the slight furrow between those expressive brows and the sudden tightening of Nic's shoulders tugged at Sasha's heartstrings. It made him want to rub the tension right out of those firm, strong shoulders.

"No. I mean yes, we do celebrate Christmas, but we have a professional designer decorate the house. The children's grandparents are coming for Sunday brunch, and this won't come close to meeting their standards."

It took a moment of struggle for Sasha not to comment on the many ways the grandparents could go fuck themselves if homemade decorations weren't fancy enough for them. It wasn't his place to make such comments about judgmental pricks with their heads up their asses. Besides, the last thing he needed right now was to alienate Nic into firing him when he was starting to bond with the kids.

"I'm sorry if I overstepped. The lawn was a recreation of Civil War events for Ben's history class. The tree started out as a probability and statistics lesson, and a discussion on climate change turned into making eco-friendly popcorn garlands. Tomorrow, I can take all this stuff down and have everything cleaned up and back as it was."

Suppressing the disappointment of spending his free weekend restoring the house to its former condition, more than anything he ached inside at the thought of removing all signs of Christmas. Before he'd decorated with the kids, the place had felt like a museum, or maybe even like walking into a hotel. No personal touches graced any of the rooms except the children's, and even those had been rather barren. What teenaged kids—tween, in Ben's case—didn't have their walls plastered with posters of rock bands, sports stars, or celebrities at the very least?

The kids themselves had seemed equally as barren and devoid of personality at first. Sasha's impression had been of some sort of Stepford children, politely introducing themselves and then disappearing into their rooms. Perfect little zombies. Fuck that shit. After a couple days feeling them out, he'd initiated a food fight at dinner that finally broke through their icy exteriors.

They'd been so sure he was going to get fired. Then he'd distracted them, pulling them into the fight and turning the event into a chemistry lesson on kinetic-molecular theory.

It felt like a step backward to take everything down, but it wasn't his house, and his illusion of being in charge of the children was only an illusion. The alpha male had returned home. Very alpha male. While said alpha rested his hands on his hips and considered Sasha's offer, Sasha's heart rate picked back up. There wasn't much he enjoyed more than being surrounded by a hot, masculine body, but being far from petite made it a challenge to find a man like that who wasn't a bear or a beefcake. Or shorter than him like Drew had been. Not that any of those were a problem, but they weren't the characteristics he found most attractive in a lover.

"Oh," Nic said. He had a somewhat surprised look on his face when his piercing emerald gaze lifted to meet Sasha's. "I thought you were a math teacher."

Sasha shrugged. "Yeah, I have a bachelor's in math from USC, but the teaching credentials for my MAT were no joke. I had two semesters of student-teaching fieldwork and passed basic skills testing and single subjects in math, science, and gifted education. Ended up substitute teaching for months before I got my first teaching position. When I got nudged out by a tenured teacher moving to my district, I got experience as a full-time caregiver. That was a plus, though. I had to tutor just about everything, so basic subject matter is pretty rote."

"Wow," Nic said, his eyebrows lifting. A flicker of pride swelled into toasty waves of gratification in Sasha, taking him by surprise. Nic was, after all, the first person who seemed impressed by Sasha's accomplishments, something even his parents couldn't claim. Nic shook his head as if clearing it and continued. "I suppose that's fine. I mistakenly assumed their studies were overlooked while the children were entertaining themselves with all this frivolous decorating."

Sasha narrowly avoided letting loose a short bark of laughter. *Frivolous?* Apparently, the kids weren't the only ones in need of breaking the ice. The image of Nic in the midst of a food fight nearly made Sasha lose control over his laugh. It was immediately followed by the image of licking sweets from that lean, tall swimmer's body, and then a groan was the sound he was suppressing.

"Not to disagree, and I do understand the importance of schoolwork, but playtime and socializing can be important too. If everything's about working, eating, and sleeping, what do we become really? Robots?"

Nic's posture immediately tensed, his expression shuttering. So much for achieving any kind of breakthrough with the iceman. "Let me be clear here, Mr. Lindsey. When I first arrived home, my instinct was to send you on your way to your next job. Perhaps that's a little too hasty, considering we never met to go over my expectations, and I doubt Percy's done much to make those clear either."

The ironic tone coupled with affection at the mention of Percy somehow softened the blow of Nic's attempt at reprimand.

"So here they are," he continued. "I expect the children's studies to be the priority. There's a reason why someone with teaching credentials was chosen to fill this position. If the children's performance in school slides or if the disruption in my household happens again, you'll be looking for other employment. Do your job as expected, and we'll get along."

A flare of indignant anger lit the center of Sasha's chest. At the same time, his belly quivered, and his cock swelled. He'd always had a people-pleasing mentality, so dominant personalities often struck a match to his sex drive. No surprise there. But fuck. It hadn't been a month and his job was already on unsteady ground.

"No worries," Sasha replied, flashing his signature boy-next-door grin. That usually worked to smooth things over when they got rough. "I'm sure we'll do more than get along."

Nic's eyebrows shot up at the suggestive sound of that assertion, and heat instantly flooded Sasha's cheeks.

"Um, I mean I'm sure we'll get along well," Sasha added. Gahhh, his mouth sometimes! He kept talking to distract Nic, and maybe himself, from any dirty thoughts. "They missed you, especially on Thanksgiving. The kids. In case you were wondering."

Guilt and disappointment settled over Nic's features like a wet sheet. Well, damn. Making Nic feel bad hadn't been his intent.

"I'm sure it wasn't a big hardship for them to do without me." He shrugged. "Couldn't be avoided anyway, and the kids are used to my schedule."

Sasha held his tongue. Though Nic sounded like it wasn't a big deal, it was obviously a big deal. He apparently assumed he didn't matter to the kids, and maybe he even believed he didn't, but it was equally clear he wanted to matter to them.

"Yes, I'm sure they understand." No sense beating the guy up over missing Thanksgiving with his family. "Kept them busy anyway. They had fun cooking Thanksgiving dinner."

"Cooking?" Nic's brow furrowed, his eyes narrowing and his hand tunneling through his hair, leaving it disheveled. Something about his adorable confusion endeared him to Sasha and made him want to rock his boat more often. "You didn't have a chef come in? Did Percy tell you about the discretionary fund?"

"Oh yes. He told me, but most of Thanksgiving enjoyment is in cooking the meal. Of course, it's also a practical way to teach them about measurements, conversions, and a bit of food chemistry."

Nic's chiseled lips parted and then closed a few times as he visibly searched for something to say. "Certainly. Very well, then." He nodded. "I'll let you get back to… the popcorn, I guess."

"May I ask about your schedule? With it being the weekend—"

"I'm working all weekend with the exception of Sunday brunch. You don't need to concern yourself with that. A chef and staff come in for the service, and your weekends are your own anyway. When I'm not at home, Percy's here to watch over the kids on weekends."

"Yes, he mentioned that." But Sasha had been spending his weekends with the kids anyway, making meals with them, helping them with homework, and playing board games with them. He wasn't sure Nic would approve, but he'd played video games with them on his own system. What kid these days didn't have some sort of gaming system, especially when funds weren't a factor?

"All right. Well, have a good evening." Nic's eyes dropped down to where Sasha twisted the edge of his T-shirt, a nervous habit left over from childhood whenever his parents had dumped him on yet another set of strangers. Sucking in a harsh breath, Nic clenched his jaw and pivoted away to jog up the curved flight of stairs to the second floor, where most of the bedrooms were.

Damn. Pretty sure he'd fucked up Nic's first impression of him. Sasha glanced down. His right hip and lower abs were on full display where his shirt had ridden up. Hmm. So had that put Nic off? Something told him that wasn't the case here, though. It wasn't like Sasha didn't recognize attraction when he saw it. In fact, closeted men would never get laid if not for intuitive men like Sasha, and he didn't even slightly believe Nic was in the closet. The man had eyed Sasha like a creamy piece of hand-dipped Christmas candy. Without a doubt, his new boss was hot for him.

What kind of hell-spawned demons haunted Sasha that he had to land his new job living in the home of a sexy gay boss? With only a few percent of the population being gay males, the odds were astronomical. The only way this wasn't ending in complete disaster was if Sasha *didn't* want to lick every inch of his boss's lean, commanding body—and yeah, he could taste the salt of Nic's skin already. There was no fucking doubt. He was truly cursed.

Chapter Five

Nic

NIC had spent all day Saturday holed up in his office across the Sound in Seattle, and then he'd stayed in his office's attached mini suite overnight. Would Percy say he was hiding away in complete avoidance? Not only would his assistant do so, but he *had* taken up nearly an hour of Nic's time with his conjectures about Nic's motivations.

Truth be told, Percy wasn't far off, but it was the anxiety gnawing at him that had kept him working more than anything else. His father and mother coming to his home for brunch this morning made his jaw clench and his stomach queasy, so eating was the last thing on his mind.

He straightened his deep plum tie and double-checked the matching cufflinks as he jogged up the steps to his front door. As he assessed the mansion's exterior, he blew out a hard breath. So far, so good. As expected, Sasha had cleared the debris from the front yard and removed the lights around all the windows. For the first time, Nic's nerves began to settle. Maybe he would feel a little better if he'd arrived home early enough to inspect the house before he expected his parents, but a delay at the helipad had made that impossible.

As he reached the door, a long town car pulled around the drive, and Nic braced himself for a hellish morning. He'd prepared something of a brief on how he'd driven Leighton Price back into high profitability this quarter and turned the company around. Okay, so that was a bit of a stretch, and he had a lot of work ahead to get even close to that goal, but his parents didn't need to know the details right now. It would only become a problem if he couldn't get enough new contracts in time to meet his father's ultimatum.

When the driver assisted them from their car, their familiar austere faces told him nothing he said would satisfy them. His mother Evelyn's dark eyes glanced over the house, her lips pinching tightly together. He opened the front door to invite them inside, and she avoided eye contact, passing a bejeweled hand over her perfectly coiffed, salon-bottled brunette hair as she pushed by him with his father following right behind.

"It's late to have no decorations up, don't you think, Nicolas?"

His teeth would surely crack with the amount of pressure he applied to them a moment before he answered. "Yes, Mother, a bit late, but I've been away on business. I have a decorator scheduled for tomorrow."

Neither of them looked his way as they handed their outerwear to him as if he were a servant. No, rather like a coatrack.

"Seems like the children could benefit from a well-run household."

"It's handled, Mother." Anything further he would have said died in his throat as they passed through the foyer and caught sight of the den. *Dear mother of God.*

His father spun to face him. "What the hell is this?"

Speechless, Nic stared at what appeared to be the aftermath of a tornado. Bottles and dishes littered the tables and carpet. At least a dozen pizza boxes were scattered around the furniture with what appeared to be an entire pizza completely flipped facedown on the carpet with a halo of splattered sauce. Board game pieces spread haphazardly around the room. If there'd been booze, underwear, and cigarette butts, Nic might have guessed his home had been invaded by a motorcycle club. But no. This was the work of unruly, unsupervised teens.

His skin grew icy, and his muscles tightened as he turned to face his parents. Of course. Now they deigned to look at him, and he hated what he saw in their eyes. As if on cue, they both pivoted and headed toward the coat closet where Nic had placed their belongings.

"Seems you're unprepared for company," his father said. "Josephine would be disgusted with how you're raising her children."

Without any further words, they walked out the door, leaving that parting shot to cleave into Nic's gut. He stumbled back against the wall and fought to catch his breath. No matter how he tried to harden himself, they always knew how to flay him open, but maybe knowing how to eviscerate adversaries was how his father had become such a successful businessman.

What Nic would never understand was how he'd become a target of his own flesh and blood.

He strode into the middle of the den and made a slow spin. Yes, the pitiful Christmas tree was gone. All the popcorn was gone. The decorations on the walls were gone. Obviously, Sasha had fulfilled his promise to remove the disruptions to Nic's home. As much as he wanted to point fingers at the manny for the mess, he really couldn't. Technically, Sasha wasn't on duty over the weekend. Even asking him to remove the decorations had been outside of the hours Nic required.

What to do about this mess, though? He'd been having trouble controlling the kids lately, but this was too much. As painful to admit as it was, his father had been right. He needed to do right by his sister and get the kids proper care, discipline, and education. Raising them himself wasn't going to give them that.

Swiping a hand down his face, Nic hit the first contact on his cell.

"Hey, Percy. Where are you, and what are you doing right now?" He paced as he listened to his friend's answer. "Good. Meet me in the den when you're done, please."

Nic hurried down the hall and across the way to the kitchen to let the chef know brunch was off, but instead of the catering team, he found another disaster area in the kitchen and a note left on the island countertop. They'd already left. Unwilling to deal with the mess and unable to locate a responsible adult, the chef and his team had abandoned the job.

Fuck.

His insides were so twisted up, he couldn't even tell what he was feeling. Was this cold, sick feeling anger? Was it despair? Maybe a combination. Heading back to the den to meet Percy, he didn't notice Sasha at first. Nic's head jerked up just in time to stop short of running right into the man's muscular back and firm, round backside.

He couldn't resist a quick dip of his gaze. Sasha's jogging pants hung low around slim hips, and Nic's eyes feasted on the upper curve of flesh revealed there. The urge to grip those globes while he pounded his hips against that tight flesh drove away the chill that had settled in Nic's chest.

Forcing his eyes up a second before Sasha turned around was fortuitous on one hand and pure torture on the other because now Nic faced Sasha's well-formed pecs, dusted with golden hair and glistening with perspiration. The formfitting tank top did nothing to hide that toned body from Nic. The scent of clean linen, evergreens, and a hint of musk filled his senses and begged him to rub his face all over that chiseled chest.

"What happened in here?" Sasha's question brought Nic back to his senses.

"You don't know?"

Sasha's jaw clenched, and suddenly Nic felt like a complete ass. He hadn't meant to accuse the man of wrongdoing, but he supposed it had sounded that way.

"I left yesterday afternoon to do some sightseeing. Spent the night on the other side of the Sound because I haven't left the island since I arrived a couple of weeks ago. Anyway, I came in through the service entrance early this morning."

Nic sighed and ran both hands through his hair. "I'm sorry. I wasn't trying to pin responsibility on you."

Something softened around Sasha's blue eyes, turning them from harsh ice to warm summer skies. "No problem." He glanced over his shoulder at the disaster area before turning back to Nic. "You know, this is a big flashing neon sign."

"What do you mean?"

With a sigh, Sasha's hands went to his hips, drawing Nic's eyes right back to them and making his mouth water. With no light effort, Nic dragged his focus back to Sasha's face, which now held the barely subdued smile of a man who knew he was being admired.

"You know how dogs get into the garbage and chew your shoes when you're away from home?"

"You're joking, right?"

"Nope. Kids act out too when they need attention."

Well, this was some bullshit. "These kids aren't neglected, Sasha. If they're acting bratty, it's because they're overindulged and need more discipline."

Sasha held up his hands. "I'm not trying to interfere, but I have a lot of experience with kids. If you could sit down with them and talk about this"—he gestured behind him—"and why it happened, maybe spend the day with them, I think you'd get better results than with punishment."

A headache throbbed at the base of Nic's skull and behind his eyes. He'd had his hands full with Leighton Price, and the last thing he needed was escalating trouble with the children. They couldn't have picked a worse time to rebel.

Yes, Sasha seemed to have a long history of working with children on his résumé, but Nic was in no mood to have yet another heap of criticism added to the pile already on his shoulders. His parents, Percy, and his own guilty conscience were enough to deal with.

"Thank you for your concern. I'm sure we'll handle everything just fine." There. That was the right tone. Not too dismissive but clear on who was in charge.

Piercing blue eyes seemed to look right into Nic, and he may as well have been naked for all he hid from the Adonis in front of him. Holy fuck, what those eyes did to his insides. The urge to fidget struck him while a gentle flutter settled into his belly. It was inexplicable. Nic directed boardrooms full of powerful men. He was smooth, calm, and cultured when meeting other commanding CEOs and influential politicians. Yet this man took him back to his late teens when he'd had his first real crush on one of his professors. Ironically, it had been his math professor.

Sasha sent Nic a curt nod before heading up the stairs toward his personal suite. Damn his eyes, he couldn't drag his gaze from that luscious backside until Sasha was no longer in sight. Of course, this would be the moment Percy showed up, the bastard.

"Get some."

"Go to hell, Percy."

"Holy shit. What the fuck happened here?" Percy weaved through the carnage in the den, pivoting his head to survey the damages. Then he looked back at Nic. "Never mind. Not like someone would break in, vandalize, and leave without stealing anything. All while the staff were home in their respective rooms. Kind of obvious who that leaves."

"Yeah." Nic entered the den, swept aside an empty chip bag and pizza box, and sat on one of the sofas. The arm was sticky where some mystery gunk had been wiped on the fabric. "They've never gone this far. It's ten times worse because it ruined our Sunday brunch, and my parents saw the mess. I haven't seen Lucy or Ben yet this morning, so they must have known it would."

"Hate to agree, but I do." His brawny assistant flopped onto the sofa across from him and propped his feet on the coffee table. Almost noon and Percy still lounged in his plaid sleep pants and loose gray T-shirt the color of his eyes. His dark hair and somewhat pale skin made him look like a vampire on a good day, but even more so against the light cream sofa. Now, he shoved that dark hair back from his creased brow, a frown on his face. "So what will you do about this?"

"Well, first things first. They need to clean all this up. Not going to have a housekeeper wiping their asses for them."

"Reasonable."

Nearly a full minute passed before Nic admitted what had been developing in the back of his head the past several weeks. This incident, more than anything, had shoved it to the forefront.

"I need a favor."

"You pay me, Nic. You don't need to call it a favor as if I have a choice or something."

He chuckled, and Percy grinned, the tension finally relaxing from his features.

"Whatever." Nic balled up the chip bag next to him and tossed it at Percy's head, but Percy dodged it with ease.

"Don't ever try out for sports."

"Too late. Where were you when I was away at school?" Nic cleared his throat. "Speaking of that, your newest task is to find a couple of the best boarding schools around. Not too far away. Keep it in Washington unless there's nothing adequate here."

Percy's eyebrows shot up, and for the first time since Nic had known him, he was speechless. Then that tension coiled right back up in his expression, and the crease in his brow returned. He opened his mouth, but

Nic already felt awful enough for considering sending the kids away to school.

"Don't," Nic said with a wave of his hand. "I know you want to argue. I've been thinking about this for a while, and it's been your voice in my head bitching at me about it the entire time."

"But this is some serious shit, Nic."

"I'm aware. For now, I only need the information. Believe me, I haven't made a decision yet. I'm not going to ship them off right now, but I have to consider it might do them good. Maybe more good than sticking around here with me. What do I know about raising kids?"

"You don't have to know everything. You don't have to be perfect. They only need quality time and attention."

"Yeah, see, that's the problem. I can't afford either of those. Hanging on to the business is taking everything right now. Maybe in a few quarters things will improve, but I'm in the middle of a battle for my seat at this company."

"Would it be so bad to lose that battle?" Percy rose from the sofa, shaking his head. "You can do better than Leighton Price. You telling me manufacturing is your grand dream?"

"Of course it's not, but it's a little late to change things. I've invested too much to give up on it."

Percy headed out of the den, making a sound reminiscent of a disapproving grandmother, which Nic ignored. "All right. I'm rounding the kids up to clean this shit. And I'll get you the info. Sometime this year."

Raising his middle finger, Nic waved his friend away. Percy's absence didn't resolve the turmoil in Nic's head. He'd been groomed from a young age to take over Leighton Price. What would he do if he didn't have that? Be a stay-at-home dad to his sister's unruly children?

You don't have to be perfect.

Not true. He'd always had to be perfect. When he wasn't, his shortcomings were inevitably rubbed in his face. At work. At home. There was no escape. So what if he did get fired as CEO?

For one shining moment, relief shook Nic to his core at the image of him free of his parents' control, free of the job he was good at but secretly despised. In the next moment, panic set in. So much of his life was out of his control, he couldn't imagine what life would look like if he got control back. Weighing the pros and cons, it was too much risk to give up his position.

Someday—when the children were grown—they would understand.

Chapter Six

Sasha

SASHA bolted upright, his face flushed with heat and the sheets clinging to his sweat-dampened skin. After a few deep breaths, his pulse finally slowed enough to hear over the pounding beat. Damn, what a dream. He slid back down into the plush bedding, savoring what he could remember of it. The weight of Nic's body pressing him into the mattress. The soft breaths and grunts as Nic thrust into him. The hands gripping Sasha's hips and teeth digging into his shoulder as if to mark territory.

If hooking up with the iceman came even halfway close to this dream, he was going to have a hard time keeping his hands off him. Not that the opportunity had been there. He hadn't seen or heard from Nic in four days, since that shitty Sunday that had wrecked the kids' dispositions for the rest of the week. Other than school and meals, they'd been relegated to their rooms. Grounded until the end of time, according to them.

Unfortunately, it had been Percy delivering the punishment. Looked like Sasha could expect to be treated like a resident babysitter, his expertise ignored. The situation was nothing new. Employers tended to be skeptical of the male perspective when it came to the care and development of children, like men couldn't possibly be great parents. The viewpoint was even further compounded once people learned he was gay, but unfortunately, the bias was often too subtle to point a finger at.

With a grunt, Sasha rolled out of bed and threw on a pair of shorts and a tank top. It was so early that the gray morning light barely tinged the sky, but he was too restless to sit around the house. Ignoring the cold, Sasha went for a run to clear his head.

Images of Nic still scalded his thoughts, no matter how much Sasha tried to expunge them. There was no doubt Nic was an ideal tall, dark, and handsome type with a dose of commanding, a potent mix in Sasha's fantasies, but he was stubborn. And Sasha's boss. Even if Nic were remotely interested in him, which certainly felt like the case, Sasha had sworn off workplace romances.

He ran until he couldn't push his body any farther and then loped up the stairs to his bathroom for a quick shower. When he'd moved here, he'd wanted a fresh start, and though he still held hopes for that, a heaviness settled in his chest. He was so damned tired. Was it so much to ask for someone to be reliable, steady, true? Was it too much to have someone to lean on instead of being the one to lift everyone else up and carry them?

Drew had only been the last in a line of failed relationships. His boyfriend before Drew had left him for being too boring when he wasn't the fun guy every hour of every day. The one before that had cheated on him. The one before him left Sasha for a man who didn't nag so much and "have so many problems." And the one before that only wanted to party constantly and had eventually caused Sasha to lose his job.

By the time he'd started dating Drew, he'd learned to keep his mouth shut when he was upset about anything and to be the upbeat, happy partner, but it hadn't mattered in the end. He'd lost Drew anyway. Maybe a long-term relationship wasn't meant to be.

Before he left his suite, he rubbed his eyes and shook his limbs out. Time to put on the fun-guy face and do what he could to teach and inspire. He laughed, a little on the humorless side, but the act alone pushed him toward a better mood.

When he got to the kitchen, he discovered he wasn't the only one up early. Lucy opened cupboard after cupboard, no doubt searching for something easy to eat.

"It looks like a poltergeist struck in here."

She whirled around, her curly hair fanning out and her hand flying to her chest. "Good lord, you scared me, Sasha."

He laughed. "Sorry. But look around you." He gestured to the open cabinets all over the kitchen. "It's a head-injury hazard up in here."

She smiled, and it barely reached her eyes. "I didn't even notice I was doing that."

"How about I make us some pancakes with strawberry topping and whipped cream? That should soothe the poltergeist."

She agreed, and they closed all the open cabinet doors together before Sasha began cooking. He decided to throw some bacon in the oven, too, because, well, bacon made everything better. Lucy didn't speak in more than monosyllables while she made the whipped cream and Sasha worked at the stove. She was one tough nugget because not many people could resist Sasha's stupid jokes. No matter what he tried, he couldn't get her out of the mood she'd been in since the past weekend.

Ben poked his head in by the time they finished cooking. "Wow. It smells good in here."

"So that's what it takes to get you out of bed before noon," Sasha said.

"Well, it is almost time to leave for school," Ben replied. The boy's hair was almost as curly as his sister's but light brown and cropped close to his head instead. Something about his lanky build said he'd look a lot like a lighter version of his Uncle Nic when he reached adulthood.

Sasha snorted. "Like school's your big motivation here."

They chuffed out a wide-eyed, somewhat reluctant laugh, as if they weren't used to their caretakers speaking so informally. He brought out a pitcher of orange juice and set a plate full of fluffy pancakes in front of each kid before sitting across from them at the small breakfast nook table adjacent to the kitchen.

"You know, it's almost the weekend. Close enough that you two should be in better spirits." Neither responded beyond some kind of noncommittal hum. Sasha cleared his throat and tried to engage them again. "What's on the agenda today? Anything after school?"

"I have a report on endangered species to work on. Borrrrring." Ben didn't even look up from his plate.

"That sounds like fun. Why do you say it's boring?"

Ben didn't answer, just sent him a flat look of disgust like Sasha had asked him the dumbest question in history. As they stood and cleared away their dishes, he studied their glum expressions, and he couldn't stand it anymore.

"How would you guys feel about taking a field trip?"

"Field trip?" Lucy frowned, a crease appearing between her fair eyebrows. "Where to?"

"Seattle."

Ben looked at Lucy and shrugged, already onboard without explanation. Lucy, on the other hand, was a little skeptical.

"Uncle Nic says we're grounded."

"Technically, you're allowed to leave for school."

She laughed, a genuine one this time. "I'm pretty sure Seattle isn't the same as school."

"Debatable. You can learn a lot in Seattle," Sasha said. "Come on. It can be educational. And fun."

"And you'll call the school? To excuse us today?" she asked.

Sasha nodded. "Of course. Don't want you to get in trouble, after all."

"Where in Seattle are we going?"

"That, young Ben, is a surprise. Go grab a warm coat. I'll call the school, and we'll head out."

For the first time since he'd decorated the house with the children, their eyes lit up with excitement, and they ran up the stairs to get ready. After making the quick call to the automated attendance system at school and calling for a driver for the trip, he settled on the sofa in the den. The new decorations had been up for a few days now. As he'd half-expected, they were mind-numbingly dull and lacking in creativity, although quite expensive looking. Suitable for an iceman like Nic.

When the kids returned, they brought color back into the room, not only with their clothing but also with their enthusiasm. This was what Sasha lived for and the best reason for him to keep his dick in his pants when it came to his employer. No way could he risk messing this job up.

When they got to the front drive, he shot a yearning glance at the garage where he'd stored his Silverado. If it weren't for the specific instructions not to use his personal vehicle to transport the kids, he would have driven them himself. Instead, they got in the back of the town car and headed toward the city. Lucy and Ben remained quiet, their heads dipped over their phones, until the car parked on the ferry to the Fauntleroy Ferry Terminal on the West Seattle side of the Sound.

"You two want to get out and stretch your legs?"

They both shrugged like twin marionettes without looking up from their screens.

"How long till we get where we're going?" Lucy asked.

"About an hour. A little less maybe." Sasha tapped his tennis shoe against Lucy's. "How often do you get off Vashon?"

She sighed and shook her head, finally setting her phone aside to meet his gaze with her green eyes, so like Nic's, only a few shades lighter. "Not often enough. It's nice here, but with the twenty-minute ferry, it takes forever to get anywhere."

"Who takes you?"

"Usually Percy. Sometimes whoever the nanny is."

"Been a lot of nannies, hmm?" he asked. She nodded, and Sasha leaned forward in his seat. "Your uncle doesn't take you?"

Ben chortled. "Yeah, right." His shoulders immediately hunched inward as if the words had been an accidental outburst.

"He used to." Lips pursed, Lucy crossed her arms over her stomach. "When we first got here—after our parents died—he spent a lot of time with us."

"So what changed?"

She tensed, and a wall seemed to close her off, her expression tight. "Who knows? Got tired of us. We're not his kids, after all, and we didn't see him much before we had to come and live with him."

"Who cares?" Ben spat. "When he's home, he bosses us around and then disappears in his office. I wish he'd leave us alone and never come around at all. Wouldn't change anything if he just stayed in Seattle."

Sasha sat back without comment. He knew how to read between the lines here. Ben needed attention, time with a caring parental figure, and a nanny—or manny, for that matter—wasn't going to cut it. It would never be a substitute for family when the kids were fully aware the care was being paid for. But it was equally obvious Nic wasn't ready to hear what the kids needed most. Even if he was, his priorities put his work ahead of family.

With a lurch, the ferry pulled to the dock, and commuters began getting into their cars. As the town car followed the line of vehicles off the ramp and continued farther and farther north, the kids grew more restless, and Sasha laughed at them.

"Hey, I asked if you wanted to stretch your legs."

Ben rolled his eyes. "Where are we going? Are we close yet?"

"Oh, aren't you cute, trying to ruin the surprise." Sasha tried to contain a laugh, but his efforts failed. The kids groaned but smiled.

Lucy copied Sasha's earlier foot nudge. "Where'd you head off to last Saturday after dismantling our awesome Christmas decorations? Know anyone around here, a boyfriend or someone?"

"Wow," he said. "Am I that obvious?"

She giggled. "No. But I did see how you were looking at my Uncle Scrooge."

"Uncle Scr—oh, I see what you did there." Heat swept over his cheeks. Hell, this girl had sharp eyes. He'd been certain the kids had both been too self-absorbed in the garland making to notice much of his first meeting with Nic. He cleared his throat. "Um, no. I mean no boyfriend or anyone. Went sightseeing at the Space Needle, Pike Place Market, and such. Saw the gum wall."

Damn straight he ignored her comment on how he'd been looking at her uncle.

"Figured you'd get the tourist stuff out of the way?"

"Yep."

"Gonna be boyfriends with Uncle Nic?"

"Gross, Luce," Ben said, still looking down at his phone screen. "I don't want to think about Uncle Nic's sex life."

"Ben!" Lucy smacked his arm, finally pulling his attention from the phone.

"Hey, you made me lose my game."

Sasha wasn't about to let his mind wander down the rabbit hole of Nic's sex life, one that had become part of his nightly dreams. He cleared his throat and clapped loudly. "Wow, look, kids. We're here."

"The zoo!" Ben's eyes widened as he pressed his face against the window. It was freaking amazing how thrilled they were to get out of the house for something besides school. Sasha would have assumed rich kids would have such opportunities all the time, so these kinds of things wouldn't be impressive to them. The depth of their reaction was gratifying.

"Yep, and the WildLights have been set up for almost two weeks. If we're here late enough, the place is going to be lit up better than that fake department store Christmas tree in our den."

"Great. Now I miss our dumb Charlie Brown Christmas tree."

"Me too, Ben," Lucy said. As lame as that little tree had been, Sasha missed it as well, but apparently only a designer-quality tree was acceptable for the Price household. He'd met plenty of that sort of snobby type of parent, but oddly, Nic didn't fit into the role. The man certainly hadn't looked at Sasha with that "better-than-you" brand of distaste that came naturally to a genuine snob, even when he'd been in his grubby loungewear or workout clothes. But then, who was Nic trying so hard to impress?

The driver swung the door open, and Sasha ushered the two kids out of the car, letting his tension melt away. It was time to channel his superpower and impart some wisdom in a fun way without his students even realizing they were learning. These kids would get into the right frame of mind to be happier and more productive before they knew what hit them.

He shoved his niggle of worry to the back of his mind. The kids were getting an education, their school absence was excused, and they weren't strictly in violation of the rules of their grounding. Certainly, it wasn't a bad thing to skip for an educational trip to the zoo to learn about endangered species for Ben's report. Nobody would even notice they were out for the day.

Chapter Seven

Nic

FURY beat at the walls of Nic's veins, pounding in rhythm with his heartbeat. He tried to keep smiling and stay relaxed and friendly with his dinner guests, trying to make it look like he wasn't stalling, but he couldn't hold dinner any longer. He would have to try to swing this client solo without the family support.

The children still hadn't arrived home. Percy had assured him they were fine and out with the manny, so there was no need to contact the authorities, but they'd never not been here. Barring a few rare extracurricular activities, the kids had always come straight home after school and then stayed home. It was unheard of for the nannies to take the kids off the island. Maybe getting out would be good for them, but in this case, they were not only grounded, but also the lack of their presence had wrecked Nic's plans.

Normally, it wouldn't matter if he had his family at dinner, but this client was from a large, traditional Italian family, someone referred by the head leather craftsman at the business he'd bought in his trip to Italy. Anselmo De Franco was a powerful man, owned a lot of large successful luxury department stores, and best of all, produced his own family line of high-end fashion products. The man had brought his wife, Rossana, and young daughter, Carina, with them to dinner.

Nic not only wanted to gain this man's trust and admiration but needed it. This was the big lead that would get Leighton Price the sales contracts required to get the numbers out of the red this quarter and save Nic's ass. But he was alone. The kids hadn't shown up, and it was clear they weren't going to show up in time.

Still, he tried to show no external signs of stress as he led the little family to the formal dining room and signaled his staff for dinner service. No way around it, the entire event was painful. He could speak business with Anselmo, but when it came to getting personal and speaking the language of family life, Nic was woefully lost. He had no life outside of Leighton Price.

Rossana and Carina hardly spoke at all, despite Nic's attempts to include them in the conversation. The only good thing about this dinner was the excellent food prepared by his personal chef and her staff. Toward the end of the meal, Mr. De Franco declined dessert, explaining that Carina had an early morning for school, so they'd need to get going. That was the final death knell.

Nic's sales were slipping away like he'd let out his own blood. Anselmo almost never did business with people he couldn't socialize with as easily as work with, and he socialized best with family men and women who he could consider part of his own extended family. Family bonds were that important to him, and as much as Nic cursed that right now, it was highly admirable.

He never had bonded with his own parents, and watching Anselmo and Rossana interact with Carina could've broken Nic's heart with longing if he let it. He would never have that with his parents.

Before they rose from their chairs, loud Christmas music blasted from the kitchen next door. Dammit. That had to be the kids, though it was unusual for them to be anywhere near the kitchen when they were home. Nic froze halfway out of his chair, an apology ready at his lips, when Carina bolted from her seat and ran right into the kitchen.

"I'm sorry. The kids must be home now. They're not usually this disruptive."

Anselmo laughed and then spoke in his deep-timbred, thickly accented English. "I'm sure 'disruptive' is included in the definition of kids. Shall we see where Carina got to?"

He didn't seem the least perturbed by the noise or by Carina's sudden departure. They rose and, following her toward the cheerful music, walked through the door adjoining the dining room to the kitchen, where it seemed like a flour bomb had gone off. The white powder was all over a few counters and sprinkled over much of the floor. The kids had splotches on their faces and clothes. Mixing bowls and measuring utensils littered the counters. Baking sheets and cooling racks waited on the long island that divided the room.

Nic had stopped inside the doorway, but the De Francos were already across the room talking to their excited daughter. Carina had already met Lucy and Ben moments before the adults had entered—perhaps learning from inclusion in her parents' social lives, she worked her charm quickly—so she introduced them to her parents.

The kids were perfectly mannered, greeting the couple, but they studiously avoided Nic. He tried to smooth the scowl from his face, but the last thing he needed was their disruption further crashing any deal he could work out with De Franco. And they damn well knew they were supposed to be grounded to their rooms right now, though he couldn't very well chastise them in front of the guests.

"What are we doing in here, Carina?" Anselmo asked.

"Making Christmas cookies. They said I could help!"

It was the most words Nic had heard from the little eight-year-old all night, and she bounced up and down as she shouted the last ones. Nic cringed, but the most amazing thing happened. Both De Francos relaxed into warm smiles and laughter, even more so than when they'd first arrived. In fact, they dove wholeheartedly into the cookie making, and Rossana volunteered to show them how to make traditional chocolate amaretti cookies.

"I can't believe how well-stocked this kitchen is, Nic," Rossana said. And he couldn't believe she was finally warming up to him enough to do more than stiffly answer his questions.

"Ah, yes. I'm not going to lie about the credit here. That's all my personal chef's doing. The secret is to hire someone who's extra obsessive about their kitchen, especially the pantry."

The kitchen became a flurry of activity, everyone mixing and measuring, laughing and singing. He'd never seen the kids smile and enjoy themselves so openly. In fact, he'd never seen anything like this kind of display of family warmth in anything but movies. Something in him locked up, holding him on the outside of it. Watching it unfold. Did people really live this way?

He took a step back, right against a solid wall of muscle. Strong hands drifted up his biceps to help recover his balance. At the same time, that familiar evergreen scent surrounded him, sending Nic's pulse racing.

"Whoa. Sorry about flying in here like that." Sasha's deep voice rumbled close to Nic's ear, and goose bumps rose over his skin in response.

When Nic turned, Sasha was inches away, those delicious lips so close yet so far. A wide smile appeared on his face, his teeth bright and even in his tanned face. Laugh lines at the corners of his eyes spoke to Sasha's cheerful personality. The man was so magnetic, Nic had to catch himself and move away before he leaned in closer to take those lips with his own or bury his face against Sasha's skin and breathe in that intoxicating scent.

"Hey, folks, I'm back with more eggs and butter. Looks like our party grew." Sasha set his grocery bag on the small bit of counter space left open near the sink, approached the De Francos, and introduced himself. Then he threw himself right into the middle of the activity like he'd never been gone. He lifted Carina onto a stool and helped her operate a cookie press.

"I never used this before. What are these, Sasha?" she asked.

"These are butter spritz cookies, and to tell the truth, you don't have to have one of these gizmos. They sure are fun, though, right?"

As he watched, Nic's chest grew tighter and tighter until it was hard to draw breath. How did Sasha do this, just jump in as if it were the easiest thing in the world? Was this how normal families interacted? If so, then Nic had been failing Josephine's memory more than he'd ever imagined.

The urge to join, to be messy and carefree, had never been so powerful, not since he'd been a child on the school playground. Despite that, his conditioning was stronger, so he observed it all at the edges of the fun, adding a snippet of conversation here and there, enough to keep up the illusion of his participation.

Maybe it was because of his intense scrutiny that he noticed Sasha's smile didn't quite reach the man's eyes. If Nic wasn't mistaken, the manny was faking the fun. Yet he was in the midst of it, driving it and making sure everyone had a good time.

Carina moved over to the next counter to help the older kids roll and cut sugar cookies, but Nic had trouble shifting his attention from the Adonis commanding the kitchen. At that moment, Sasha's gaze lifted from the baking sheet in front of him and met Nic's. A shock of energy shot through Nic, followed by a wave of heat.

A real smile crossing his face, Sasha tipped his head, beckoning Nic closer. "Wanna try?"

Nic shrugged and drew nearer until he stood next to Sasha, still relishing the eye contact. "I don't need to. I enjoy watching them having a good time. It's been a while. Too long."

"I'm glad I could help." Sasha took Nic's hand and placed the press in his palm. "But you're not getting out of this scot-free. Press some cookies."

Taking a deep breath, Nic eyed the cookie press and then the baking sheet. He pursed his lips and aimed the end toward the sheet. Before he could pull the lever to dispense the dough, Sasha reached in front of Nic's body, his arm against Nic's abs, and the muscles there quivered at the contact. Sasha's hand covered his, guiding it.

"Hold it straight." His voice was low and gruff, his breath warm against Nic's throat, and Nic tried not to let his thoughts turn sexual. It had been a lost cause before Sasha had first touched Nic. "Make sure the end is touching, right up against the sheet. Then press."

With that, Sasha put pressure against Nic's thumb, stroking it down the length. Nic paused and then lifted the press, leaving a perfect spritz cookie behind. As he looked down at it, a burning sensation grew at the corners of his eyes until he blinked it away.

"This is the first Christmas cookie I've ever made—the first cookie, actually."

Sasha's hand moved to the small of Nic's back. "I'm glad I could help," he murmured.

The smile was gone from his face, his friendly expression replaced by a fiery intensity Nic would never have expected from someone as sunny as Sasha. Suddenly, Nic was all too aware of his tight body brushing against Nic's thigh, hip, and shoulder. Sasha was the perfect height to tuck down right under Nic's chin, and a momentary fight played out in his head before he finally resisted the impulse to pull Sasha in.

A burst of high-pitched giggles brought Nic's attention back to his surroundings. When he looked around the kitchen, the De Francos were saying their goodbyes to the kids. Both Ben and Carina had frosting on their faces and clothing in addition to the flour.

Anselmo approached as Nic forced himself to get a few feet of distance from Sasha, who tossed the spritz cookies in one of the ovens and began herding the children to clean up the mess.

"Nic, this has been a joyful night." The older man's smile narrowed his almost hawklike golden eyes but in a warm, friendly way. "You were perhaps hoping to talk business before the night ends, but as it's late, I need to get the little one to bed. Why don't we just skip the pitch, yes?"

Nic's eyes widened. "Certainly. Where would you like to go from here?" He held his breath, his jaw clenching in anticipation. Did the man mean what Nic thought he meant?

"Let's set up a meeting to hammer out timelines and other such details. Have a good night, Nic, and thank you for dinner. You have a wonderful family, and I'm honored to have been included this evening." Anselmo walked toward the door but turned back as Nic followed. "It looks like you have some work cut out for you with this mess, so we'll see ourselves out. And there's no need to bite nails, young man. We'll set a contract for what you proposed as long as you can handle the volume."

With a dry laugh, he patted Nic's arm and guided his family out of the kitchen. After they cleared the door, Nic practically wilted, dropping onto a bar stool at the center island as the tension fled his body.

Sasha squeezed Nic's shoulder as he passed. "You doing okay there?"

"Sure. A long night, that's all." Nic checked his watch. They'd been baking for nearly two hours. Somehow, the time had flown. "Kids, head to bed. You've got an early morning."

They grumbled, but it seemed cleaning the kitchen wasn't as appealing as going to their rooms. Both kids threw their arms around Sasha at the same time. Nic's gaze followed them to the door.

Ben sailed through, but Lucy turned. "Good night, Uncle Nic," she said almost as an afterthought. Ben repeated the sentiment from the hallway outside, reminded by Lucy's words.

He couldn't stop staring at the door after they left. They used to hug him often when they'd first arrived four years ago. When had they grown so far apart from him? Why had they?

The clatter of metal pulled Nic's focus back to Sasha.

"You can leave those. I'll have house staff clean up in the morning," Nic said.

Sasha heaved a sigh of what could not be mistaken for anything but relief. "Thank God."

"But we do need to talk before you're done for the night."

"Well, I'm not sure that sounds good."

Nic shrugged. "I can't decide either."

"Maybe start with the problem first." Sasha leaned against the center island next to where Nic rose from the stool to face him.

"All right. I'm pretty unhappy the kids weren't home from school on time today. I had plans for a family dinner that were ruined because of it. Where were they?"

Hands moving to his hips, Sasha dropped his chin and shook his head. "I'm sorry. I didn't know about your plans for them. We were at the zoo."

"The zoo?" Nic frowned. There was no way they could get from school to the zoo and back during Seattle rush hour unless all they did was ride in the car, turn around, and ride back. He crossed his arms as the facts became obvious. "They missed school."

A harshly spoken statement, not a question.

"Yes, but I called the school so it wouldn't be unexcused," Sasha said. He lifted his head and spread his hands as if to entreaty Nic's empathy. "Ben needed to research endangered species for a report due Monday, so we took a few premier tours. He got to see and learn about several species up close."

Nic waved a hand as if brushing the explanation aside. "I haven't given you authority to keep the kids home, and I won't. They aren't homeschooled, and their grades are disgraceful. They can't afford to miss days. I thought Percy shared their grade reports with you."

"He did, but—"

"I'm sure you have reasons you believe are good ones, Sasha, but it doesn't matter. I don't want them missing school for any reason barring health reasons. Do you understand?"

"I do. Really, I understand. If this is what you've decided, I'll follow your wishes from now on. But did you see how happy they were? Ben was actually excited about doing his report. He had half of it done by the time we got back from the zoo."

"And Lucy? Did she happen to have some desperate need to be at the zoo as well?"

Sasha had the nerve to grin. "Yeah, actually, she did. She has a debate coming up at the end of next week. It's about the global impact of human activity."

A burst of laughter escaped Nic. "Fuck, you're good."

"More than you know."

The look of mischief on Sasha's face and slight curve of his lips sparked a fire in Nic's belly, and he couldn't help stepping a little closer to the source of his attraction, couldn't look away from those deep blue eyes.

"On the other hand, I never could have pulled off that sale with the De Francos if it weren't for this happy catastrophe in the kitchen." He cleared his throat. "I guess I could forgive everything today because of that alone. Just this once."

"Got it. Just this once."

A moment of silence passed that carried the heavy atmosphere of the air before a thunderstorm. The faint brush of Sasha's breath on his lips pushed Nic over the edge, and he closed the distance to Sasha's mouth.

At last. After nearly a week of fantasizing, he now knew how those lips felt—soft and yielding under his. Sasha firmly gripped Nic's waist, fingertips digging into muscle, pulling him even closer until they were flush. Nic bent his knees slightly, bringing Sasha's cock right against his.

A loud groan escaped him when he felt how hard Sasha was for him, and he couldn't help moving against that rigid length. Sasha's soft moan galvanized Nic. He ground against Sasha, sliding his hands over Sasha's firm ass and squeezing. Touching his tongue to the seam of Sasha's lips, Nic pressed in to deepen the kiss. The wet heat inside Sasha's mouth gave him a contact high of epic proportions. Thoughts departed, leaving only pure sensation.

The sound of their kiss, the rustle of clothing, and seesawing breaths drove his desire even higher. Sasha traced Nic's spine, making him shiver with need. He wanted to bend Sasha over the counter and thrust into his ass until the man came all over Nic's hand. The image made him nearly savage, and he bit Sasha's bottom lip, lightly scraping his teeth over it before sucking and releasing it.

"Fuck," Nic said, breaking the kiss to drag in precious air. Maybe he shouldn't have spoken because it broke the spell. Sasha regained his senses, stepping back and turning away from Nic.

"Yeah, fuck is right." Sasha blew out a breath and braced both arms on the counter as he regained his composure. "That probably wasn't the best idea."

Despite a flash of regret for the interrupted passion, Nic had to agree. Sasha was an employee, something of a troublesome one at that. Getting involved, even for a quick tumble, would be a monumental lapse in judgment. But goddamn, it would be one hell of a mind-blowing lapse. A single hot kiss already had him twisting inside with barely contained lust. Who knew how a hard fuck would mess with his head?

"No. You're right." He couldn't bring himself to look at Sasha's face. "It was a slip. We'll keep it professional."

Sasha murmured a vague agreement and slipped quietly out the door. The sudden silence bit into Nic like a burr under his skin. It had never bothered him before, but after the boisterous festivities, the silence seemed like a pointer toward something missing.

Keep it professional. Something told him there was only one way to do that. He'd have to avoid being alone with Sasha. If only it were that easy, though. They were living together, after all.

Chapter Eight

Sasha

THE air was nippy, but incredibly, the sun was shining, which Sasha understood was a rarity in Seattle this close to winter. He'd planned to spend most of his free Saturday at the Seattle Art Museum to avoid inclement weather, but as an addict of outdoor activities, he had to take advantage of the clear skies.

It turned out to be one of his better decisions. Alki Beach had some of the best cityscape views of Seattle, hands down, and it was the perfect lighting for photography. He wasn't anything close to professional, but his skills and camera were on par for some high-quality, high-resolution stock photos. Though he didn't make enough from his uploads to live on, it paid a few bills. And it certainly wasn't a tedious way to earn extra cash.

As he walked, exploring away the daylight hours, he couldn't keep his job out of his head. He'd see something the kids would love, and his mind would be right back on Vashon with them. His favorite had been the six-foot Statue of Liberty replica. Who knew this little gem was way out here in West Seattle? He'd never heard of anything like it. He retrieved his phone and nearly called Lucy to ask if they'd ever been to Ellis Island. Then he reined himself in. A little over three weeks with them, since right before Thanksgiving, and his boundaries were already blown.

Had he ever gotten attached so quickly to his other students? Maybe that was the problem. He had to stop thinking of Lucy and Ben as students. Nic had made the point clear that he wasn't there to homeschool them.

Of course, thoughts of Nic had been rolling around the back of Sasha's mind all day, but now they came right to the forefront. That scorching kiss had haunted his dreams, but it was before, when they were making cookies, that got to him more.

When he'd walked in, Nic had stood frozen on the sidelines, his body unusually tense. Sasha couldn't see Nic's face, but he didn't need to. So perhaps it wasn't much of an accident that he'd "run" into Nic when he came in. The man needed a hug, and he'd thought physical contact might bring him back into the moment. The mindfulness technique worked only for a few minutes before Nic started to tense up again, something inside winding him tighter and tighter.

He'd seen this before. Many times, actually. On holidays, there had always been children who weren't allowed to celebrate for one reason or another. They stood at the periphery with such yearning in their eyes. That had been Nic on Thursday night. He had wanted so badly to be a part of things, but something had held him back. But what could that have been? Nic was rich and powerful, authoritative and in charge of his own household. He'd had no trouble letting Sasha know how he wanted things.

He was glad he'd eventually pulled him in. To his endless surprise, nothing had felt better in years than when Nic made his first Christmas cookie. The way that man looked at him afterward had branded him, reached so far past his organs, it touched his soul and left a mark. And that, more than anything, had made their kiss that night so much more than a kiss. When he'd gone to bed later, it was Sasha who'd been consumed by yearning.

Nothing could be more dangerous than that. He was too attached to those kids already, and it would chew him up to have to leave because he'd screwed up a personal relationship at work. He had no other choice but to stay away from Nic as much as possible, no matter how attracted and fascinated he was with his boss. His heart couldn't take another move.

It was obvious Sasha needed to settle down with a man and have kids of his own. He'd never wanted to admit the dream because it had seemed so impossible— not so much the having kids part but the finding a soulmate and partner in life part of it.

With a heavy sigh, he tucked his camera away. The light was getting low, the skies grayer as the hours passed, and he'd promised himself to find a place to chill and meet new people. He needed someone to get his mind off the temptation of his new boss.

An online friend from Cali had recommended Pony and said to get there early, during happy hour, because the place got crowded, especially on event nights. Sasha caught a Lyft and headed to Capitol Hill, barely registering the scenery as it passed. As much as he wanted to find the beginnings of a meaningful relationship tonight, running into someone as compelling as Nic would be an impossible task. The attraction between them had been more instantaneous and supercharged than any other first impression Sasha had experienced.

At first sight, the bar seemed like a total dive. There was nothing glitzy about the neighborhood, and the bar itself was a plain, small black building with no more than the logo of a running horse on the sign. At least the décor was interesting. Some rather large cock and balls hung from the ceiling, graffiti from hilarious to outright vulgar graced the walls, and the bathroom prominently featured a glory hole. Turned out Pony was amazing, though. Good music, good food, and plenty of good-looking men trying to chat him up. He had a few decent conversations but soon made his exit from each one. He wasn't feeling it tonight, and call him emotionally needy, but he'd never been one of those guys who could hook up with strangers.

Before it got too crowded, Sasha got a prime seat at the bar where he could people watch with abandon, and then a tall, broad figure took the last seat at the bar next to him.

"Hey, make any new friends?"

That voice jerked Sasha around in his seat, his head swiveling to the newcomer.

"What do you know?" he said with a laugh. "Nearly a million people in this city. I can't imagine the odds of running into you here. How're you doing, Percy? I thought you were with the kids on weekends."

His stomach flipped as he imagined Nic hanging out around the house with the kids over the weekend. He was usually a ghost, almost always working out of his Seattle office or holed up in his home office.

"Nah. Nic got a drop-in sitter for them. He's in town working on the contracts for the De Franco deal. That's actually how I got stuck here."

"Lucky you."

The grimace on Percy's handsome face told him exactly how the guy felt about it. Sasha rather liked Percy, though his first impression had been of a cold contract assassin who'd kill you in a hundred horrible ways if you looked at him sideways. The guy was actually quite laid-back, but he had a military-style cut, a little longer on top, huge muscles, and a tall, dominating physique. That imperious quality appealed to Sasha in a mad, mad way, but his preference went toward a leaner build. *Like Nic.* He shook the thought away as quickly as it appeared.

"It's what happens when you work for Nic," Percy said. His sudden grin took the bite out of his words. "You'll get used to getting sucked in. He lives for work, so he forgets not everyone operates the same way. Just don't let him steamroll you because I guarantee he'll try a few times."

"I take it this isn't just a busy time for him right now."

Percy shook his head. "Nope. Sorry to say."

"I didn't realize you, uh...." He waved a hand toward the crowd behind them.

"Yeah, well, I do surprise a lot of people. It's the most fun when I show up to a business dinner with a man on my arm instead of someone with tits and a vagina." Percy chuckled, his white teeth flashing in the dim light.

"It was like hitting a jackpot to find Nic to work for. He doesn't give a flying fuck who my dates are, and he's as out as I am. I guess from the outside, it might be hard to tell with Nic, too, though."

That hit Sasha right in the curious bone. "What do you mean?"

Percy studied him a few moments before answering, and Sasha had never felt more like squirming in his seat as he did so.

"I'd say he has a 'don't shit where you eat' philosophy. He doesn't date business associates or employees. He doesn't even date people here in the city and doesn't frequent the clubs here." He leaned on the bar and took a long drink of his beer. "To my knowledge, he only hooks up when he's out of the area."

Sasha looked down at the bar coaster he'd been toying with and then spun his martini glass. "Makes it kind of hard to maintain a relationship, doesn't it?"

A huff of cynical laughter was Percy's immediate response. "Like he has time for that. I've tried for years to talk sense into that bastard. It wouldn't kill the business if he took more personal and family time, but he won't slow down for anything. I'm worried he'll work himself into an early grave. Plus...."

Twisting around, Sasha angled toward Percy, who'd disappeared into some internal debate. "Plus what?"

"Plus, I think something happened a while back, right before you got here." He shook his head and frowned. "He's been more preoccupied and obsessed than usual about profits lately. I'm used to him telling me everything. Too much. Way too much." He laughed a second before continuing. "Now, it's like he's locked himself behind a wall."

Something about that reminded Sasha of Nic's reaction to the Christmas cookie baking, when Nic'd had the appearance of standing behind a wall that kept him from joining in. Guess the man had a lot more walls to go around.

"Hey, uh, incoming on our six." The edge of alarm in Percy's voice pulled Sasha out of his thoughts. Why the hell would Percy, of all people, be nervous about getting hit on? From the corner of his eye, movement drew attention to two nice-looking guys approaching with intent written all over their faces.

"Okay, roll with me a little."

With that, he reached up and stroked the side of Percy's close-cut hair. It was surprisingly silky, making it a concerted effort not to take advantage of the situation and stroke his friend's hair again. Then he smiled enticingly and rubbed Percy's thigh. The stunning smile of gratitude Percy sent him was difficult to look away from, but he did turn enough to see the two men drop their shoulders and give up on their mission.

"Wonder what made them think we weren't into a four-way," Percy said. He clapped his hand on Sasha's back. "Thanks, man. You have no idea how much I appreciate that."

"You're obviously not here to hook up."

"Nope. Just needed fresh air and a drink before heading home. I'm kind of a regular since it's only a mile walk to get here." He studied Sasha again, apparently approving of what he saw and deciding to elaborate. "People take one look at me and make assumptions about what kind of man I am. They're almost always wrong. Neither of those guys were what I need or want."

It took only a second to analyze what had happened in light of Percy's words before Sasha figured it out. "I'm sorry."

A confused look furrowed Percy's brow. "For what?"

"I did the same thing."

He laughed. "It's okay, Sasha. You know now, so when you run into any good, hard, sexy tops who could handle me, maybe you can send them my way. That's harder to find around here than you'd think."

"Nic never appealed to you?"

"No, no, no, and absolutely no." Percy gave a decisive shake of his head. "First, he's my boss. Second, he's my best friend—"

"I hear a romance novel or two in there somewhere."

He laughed and then continued, ignoring the comment. "And third, he's not strong enough to pin me the way I like."

"Well, there's the deciding factor."

"Goddamn, Sasha, why do you have to need a top? You're so fucking charming and funny. Are you at all vers?"

"Nah. Anyway, I may have more muscle mass than Nic, but you've got me beat. I still couldn't pin you."

"Hell." He patted Sasha's shoulder, wordlessly reassuring him that the flirting was in jest. "I'm heading out, back to Vashon. Are you staying in the city overnight or could you use a ride home? I have the helo tonight if you'd like a bird's-eye view of the city and the Sound."

Sasha leaped up from his stool, about as excited as Ben was when they'd gone to the zoo the other day. He'd never been in a helicopter before and never imagined he'd ever get to ride in Nic's.

"I take it that's a yes." Percy tried to hide his smile, but the attempt wasn't very effective.

"It's all right. You can laugh at me all you want. Won't make me enjoy this any less."

"Yeah, I'm pretty sure that smile will take a week to pry off your face." Percy led the way out of the bar to the town car he must have sent for a while ago. "We have to get back to our building where the landing pad is. Won't be long, though. The pilot's already standing by."

"A pilot, huh?" Sasha asked as they rode from Capitol Hill to the Price building in downtown proper. "Is he cute?"

"*She* is quite cute. Just not sure she's your type."

Covering his face with his hands, Sasha groaned. "Ah, I'm a dick. That was a rather sexist assumption, huh?"

Percy patted Sasha's thigh right above his knee. "Don't sweat it. Most of the pilots are male, and Lorna knows that. I'm sure she wouldn't take offense to it."

The helicopter ride captivated Sasha with the incredible nighttime panorama of the city. The sparkling lights, towering buildings, whitecaps on the dark waves—all of it took his breath away. As they'd pulled farther from land, the cars shrank until they were tiny toys in the distance. The best part was Lorna. She was a complete sweetheart, endeared with Sasha's enchantment with the flight. Maybe taking it as a chance to show off, she banked and swooped often. Sasha cheered her boldest moves.

By the time they finally landed on the helipad, they were all laughing. Lorna took off again shortly after. She lived in one of the suburbs around Seattle with her boyfriend and his three-year-old daughter. She promised to take him out whenever she was on shift and they both had the time.

He split ways with Percy at the stairs, Percy's suite being the only one on the first floor. As he climbed the steps, it occurred to him that there'd been no tiresome effort on his part tonight. With Percy, anyway. It wasn't easy to be the fun party guy with all the jokes and charisma, especially now.

Two years away from thirty, he never thought he'd still be so lost, alone. He should have been settled into a career by now, with a husband he could start a family with. Fuck, he didn't even have a home of his own, and after getting screwed over by Drew, his finances were a shit show.

A petite little body crashed into him with a sharp yelp, yanking him out of his bout of self-pity. He reached out instinctively, balancing Lucy on her feet.

"Oh shit. I'm sorry. Are you okay, Lucy?"

"I'm all right. Don't apologize. I'm the dummy who bolted out of the room without looking." She kept her head down, her curly golden hair covering most of her face.

Something was wrong. Lucy never hunched her shoulders like this. She had the same commanding personality her Uncle Nic had. Before she could slink downstairs, Sasha cupped her chin and tilted her head up. She resisted for only a second, her good manners not allowing much in the way of defiance.

Her eyes were puffy and her nose slightly rosy.

"What happened? You wanna talk about it?"

"It's just a little cold." Her voice faltered.

"Nope. That's not a cold," Sasha said. "Want some hot chocolate made the old-fashioned way?"

"What way is that?"

"The way that requires real chocolate and no packets of powder."

She gave him a real smile and nodded. They went downstairs to the kitchen where Lucy sat on one of the stools while Sasha pulled out chocolate, milk, cream, sugar, and vanilla. He gave her time to relax while he began mixing and heating everything in the saucepan. It wasn't until he began chopping up the chocolate bars that he spoke.

"So, was the sitter cute?"

She burst into laughter, caught off-guard by the unexpected question. "I guess if you're into the geriatric types. I don't know why Uncle Nic insists we need guardians anymore."

"Hmm." He rubbed his stubbly chin with the back of his hand. "Probably worried about you. That's usually why people can't let go of childhood rules."

Lucy's derisive snort made him smile. It seemed too indelicate for such a delicate girl. He whisked the cream mixture, removed it from the heat, and added the chocolate pieces, stirring until it was thoroughly melted and creamy. He poured the beverage into two mugs, sat next to Lucy, and watched her have a chocolategasm over her drink.

"God, you need to bottle this. You'd make a fortune," she said, her eyes nearly rolling back as she sipped the thick liquid.

"I'll keep that in mind after I get fired from this job."

She smacked his arm. "Don't even joke. I'd boycott this house if Uncle Nic ever got rid of you."

"Ah, so life *is* good after all. Then, why were you crying?"

Her eyes narrowed on him, too smart to not see how she'd been maneuvered into a better mood. She must have decided she like the better mood, though, because she finally started talking.

"I loved what we did the other day, making the cookies and earlier at the zoo and everything. Even you making us do our homework didn't ruin the day for us."

She stopped, her gaze dropping to the mug between her hands.

"I see. I'd cry about that too."

Sasha cupped his hands over hers in a gesture of empathy, trying his damnedest to keep a straight, serious face.

"Stop it," she said with no heat in her words. She laughed and turned her hands over to grip his. "It made me miss Mom and Dad, that's all. We used to do stuff like that all the time, but when we came here, things were so different. It feels like everything good drained out of our lives. I thought I'd never feel like that again, the way we used to be when Mom and Dad were alive."

He squeezed her hands. "I'm sorry it hurt you."

"I didn't mean—"

"If you're about to backtrack, forget about it. What I'd like to know instead is what about doing all that fun stuff hurts?"

A thoughtful look crossed her features, and then her pale jade gaze met his. "I was thinking we'd never get to do anything like this with them again. Their absence hurt."

He sighed and pursed his lips. "Would it help to think about it all a little bit differently?"

"Like how?"

"Maybe instead of focusing on their absence, you can try to remember them, remember doing these kinds of things with them. Think of what they would do if they were there with you. Make it a way to be closer to them."

Her brow furrowed, and her lips tightened while she tried not to cry again. "I would love that," she whispered. "I'll try. Can we do more stuff like that?"

"Yes, of course. As long as your uncle allows it."

A frustrated breath blew the curls away from her cheeks. "Great. That means no."

"Why so?"

She tipped back the last of her chocolate and set the cup down with an aggravated click. "He used to be different. You know, when he came over to our house. He had more fun, and he treated us like we were people who mattered. It's changed now. We're another responsibility in a long list for him. I don't think he ever wanted us." She shrugged. "I guess that's fair. He hasn't had children for a reason, and I'm sure he never expected to have us to care for."

"Trust me, I can tell he loves you. I'm sure he's only preoccupied with business issues right now."

She rolled her eyes. "*For four years?* It's okay. I can deal with it, but Ben's another story. He's younger, and he was little when we moved here. It's harder for him. I try to make up for it, but Sasha, I'm not a mom. I don't know how to be one."

He pulled her into a hug. "You don't need to be one, young lady. You are, however, one hell of an amazing older sister."

After sending her off to bed and taking care of their dishes, Sasha headed to his own suite, his mind buzzing. Today was supposed to relax him, not get him all tied up in more knots. Talking to Lucy had made it painfully clear the kids needed more from Nic than they were getting, but Nic was too focused on work to see that.

Ironically, it was equally clear Nic needed them as much as they needed him. Those imaginary walls surrounding him had to come down if the man was ever going to experience real happiness, but Percy had already tried and failed to get Nic to notice. How the hell was Sasha supposed to help, especially when he was supposed to stay away from Nic?

Fuck if that didn't give Sasha yet another restless night.

Chapter Nine

Nic

HE'D only made it three days before his quest to avoid Sasha crashed and burned. He should have known Sasha's work with the kids would eventually necessitate the proximity, but today's reason had been a surprise because they rarely needed Nic for homework help. However, Sasha had brought Ben to his office to enlist him for a family tree project, which is how he'd ended up with Sasha and Ben, standing around the dining room table where an enormous poster board and stack of construction paper lay. Once Sasha got them started, Nic with the names and Ben with the tree leaves, the quiet became unnerving and let him focus too much on the man across the table from him.

Normally, Sasha wouldn't have been around while the rest of the family had Sunday brunch with Nicolas Senior and Evelyn Price, but Nic's parents hadn't even bothered canceling personally. They'd had one of their assistants leave a curt voicemail Saturday afternoon informing Nic they wouldn't be available until the Christmas party they hosted at their own estate. Their disapproval of him couldn't have been any clearer.

"You okay?" The warm brush of Sasha's hand along Nic's forearm made goose bumps rise in its wake. His eyes met and held Sasha's for a few moments too long to be considered casual. He couldn't help himself. Sasha's eyes were magnetic and had their own gravity. Looking into those bright blues plucked a cord that connected to some forgotten place buried deep inside Nic, and that strum of sensation felt so damned good.

"I'm fine." As much as he wanted to swim in the feelings Sasha brought out in him, it wasn't helping his decision to curb his attraction to him—even though his head went pleasantly fuzzy at Sasha's concern. In the past, only Percy had been able to tell when Nic was distressed, and Percy had known him for years. He turned his attention back to Ben's project. He'd nearly finished drawing the diagram of the family lineage, going back a few generations, when Sasha leaned closer to read it.

"Ben, your ancestry looks like it would have papers from a breed association," Sasha said.

His nephew's snorting laughter turned into outright guffaws. Nic couldn't have predicted he'd ever use the word *guffaw* in his life, but Ben hadn't laughed this hard in years.

"Hey, why's that so funny?" he asked.

Ben straightened from where he hovered over the construction paper on the table. "I pictured Grandmother and Grandfather on leashes being paraded around a ring and posed for the judges."

Just like that, the image flashed in his head, and he had to laugh too. "Thanks a lot. I'm never going to keep a straight face when I look at them again."

While Nic had filled out all the names and drawn a diagram of the Price family's most recent ancestry, Ben had almost finished cutting out multicolored leaves. Sasha stood over the poster board and used watercolor markers to create a large tree, with branches widespread, in the center of the poster board and began filling in details and shading. The strokes bold and precise and colors flawlessly blended, the poster could have been an art piece.

"Wow, Sasha." Staring at the tree, Ben stopped his scissors halfway around the edge of a leaf cutout. "You're an artist?"

Sasha paused and lifted his head to shoot a surprised look at Ben. "Uh, no. It's only kind of a hobby—drawing, painting, crafts."

Nic slid over and stood next to Sasha for a better view, trying to ignore the phantom heat from Sasha's muscular body. "This is amazing, Sasha. I can't believe you did this in just a few minutes."

Sasha ducked his head but failed to hide his flushed cheeks as he fanned the poster board to help dry the painting. The unexpected bout of shyness hooked Nic in the gut. Had no one noticed and complimented his artwork before? Before Nic could think twice, he slid his hand to the small of Sasha's back, the urge to soothe too strong to deny. The man was a beacon of sweet and hot at the same time, always ostensibly lighthearted, but something melancholy took over when he thought no one was watching.

"It really is incredible. I'd love to have half your talent."

"Thank you." Sasha glanced at Nic, his cheeks coloring even more. How much of a bastard was Nic that his mind went straight to sex at the sight of that blush? The play of muscles beneath Nic's fingertips sent sparks up his nerves, and his mouth went dry. Sasha's gaze lowered to Nic's mouth the moment he wet his lips, and that show of interest lit Nic up with a craving for more contact and pumped blood straight to his groin.

Reluctantly, he dropped his hand and shifted away, ignoring the sense of disappointment that followed. He'd only meant to comfort him, not start something he wouldn't allow himself to finish. Sasha seemed to become aware of his surroundings, clearing his throat and leaning back over the painting. He prodded a few spots.

"I think it's dry enough," Sasha said. "Your leaves ready, Ben?"

Ben answered, and the two of them continued with the project, securing the leaves to the poster board in the appropriate places. Sasha worked well with Ben, always providing the right direction and the right words and making him laugh without effort. Getting to such a comfortable place with Ben had never seemed so far out of Nic's reach, and a pang of regret struck hard. He grew more and more tense as he listened halfheartedly, but it was clear he had nothing to contribute beyond the information Ben had needed to fill out the leaves. Finally, he couldn't take another minute of standing there frozen while his insides churned with the unbearable self-doubts he only had around the kids. He needed solace in work, the only thing he wasn't incompetent at.

"It looks great, Ben."

Ben didn't acknowledge him at first, apparently forgetting Nic was there. No surprise. Nic was still waiting for the day it wouldn't bother him to be so insignificant.

"Oh. Thanks, Uncle Nic."

"You're welcome. I'll be in my office working for a while if anyone needs anything."

"Really?" Sasha asked, his head jerking up. At seeing Nic's raised eyebrow, he continued. "You're working on a Sunday?"

"I got a little behind on emails while I was in Italy. It's a good day to catch up."

"Oh?" Sasha arched one golden eyebrow. "Emails. From over a week ago?"

Nic shrugged. Obviously Sasha didn't buy Nic's excuse. He glanced down at the poster and then at Nic, his jaw clenching and unclenching. Whatever he was thinking, he was either uncertain how to say it or uncertain whether he should. He shifted on his feet and then nodded. "I guess it is a good day to catch up. Will you be done by dinnertime?"

He wanted Nic around? Well fuck. That's what the strange behavior was about. Sasha didn't want him to retreat to his office. A spike of pleasure curled through him. He fought the impulse to step right up to Sasha and kiss the hell out of him. Unfortunately, he wasn't successful at keeping his thoughts from showing on his face. Sasha's expression tightened, the heat in his eyes showing Nic how onboard he was with those thoughts.

The clatter of Ben knocking over the glue gun reminded Nic they weren't alone. Good thing too. Nic's willpower was woefully absent in the face of Sasha's appeal. Forbidden fruit had never been more tempting.

"I should be done by six," he answered, barely remembering Sasha had posed a question.

He made his escape—having no illusions that it *was* an escape—and buried himself in work. The deal with Anselmo had nearly brought him to his sales goals for the quarter, but he needed to come up with a few more strategies to either cut costs or nail down more sales contracts. His father wouldn't settle for meeting a goal rather than exceeding it.

COMBING his email for leads, he found a few promising responses he forwarded to his sales team. As he worked his way down the queue, he reached a memo from the board sent two days earlier. That was unusual. The email should have routed to his priority folder to be reviewed right away instead of to the regular inbox. Obviously he'd been too distracted lately, and responsibilities suffered when that happened.

As he read, his blood pressure skyrocketed, and he gripped the edge of his desk. A familiar frustration climbed the back of his throat, begging for expression, something he'd never allowed himself. The damned board—led by his father, no doubt—had approved and created an audit committee. Fuckers hadn't convened a scheduled meeting so Nic could be present for the deliberation and vote.

Adrenaline flooding his veins made him jittery, and he launched from his seat and paced in front of the tall, wide window behind him. On the surface, the creation of an audit committee was a positive thing. Any company concerned about optimizing operations and growth would want such a committee.

Nic, however, knew his father better than that. There were only two reasons Nicolas Senior would want an audit committee. The biggest one was simply to show the extent of his lack of trust in Nic, grinding his censure in as deeply as he could. The most worrisome reason, though, was that having an audit committee was a requirement for a company to go public. Did his father intend to file an IPO?

When Nic had started at the family business, he never would have imagined his father opening the company to public trading on the stock market, diluting the family's control. Now? The man had already threated Nic's seat as CEO. Who knew what the hell he was willing to do? Nic just wished he knew why he'd never been good enough for his parents. Sometimes he felt the weight of a giant target on his back and a permanent bruise sinking all the way to his soul from all the hits to that target. The shining light in his life when he was growing up had always been Josephine, though his parents had eventually separated them, sending him to boarding school while she went to live with their aunt. Though he'd hated the distance, Josie had been happier there, so he couldn't entirely regret it. If anyone knew the kind of pain his parents could inflict without a single touch, it was Nic. He would have done anything to protect Josie from that.

She'd married well, pleasing even their parents when she'd said yes to Daniel, a good man from—incidentally—a wealthy family. They'd saved all their barbs for Nic, somehow deducing he wasn't going to provide the heirs they'd always expected of him. It had been somewhat of a blessing he hadn't needed to come out to his parents. They'd probably known from the time he was a preteen, right around the time they'd sent him away. Strangely, that knowledge didn't change his relationship with his parents. They'd always disapproved of him.

The alarm on his phone blared, making him flinch. It was almost time for dinner. Shit. He'd forgotten to let Vicki know he'd need meals for today. Grilled cheese was really the only thing he could manage to cook on his own. Hopefully, the kids would be satisfied with that, or else they'd be stuck with cold sandwiches.

He closed the office door behind him and turned straight into Lucy.

"Whoa!" She grabbed his biceps at the same time he caught her elbows.

"Careful. Where are you going in such a hurry?" he asked.

She patted him and smoothed the sleeves of his button-up as if he were the child. "To get you. It's time for dinner."

His brow creasing, he opened his mouth to ask more, but she spun and hurried away, curling her finger in a beckoning motion for him to follow. Dinner? Since when did they fetch him for dinner? Opportunities for the three of them to eat together—apart from the dreaded Sunday brunches—had always come as pleasant coincidences. At least the last few years. It'd been almost too painful for them to all be in the same room when Lucy and Ben first came to live with him, the collection of their sorrow weighing more on Nic than when he was alone.

No wonder they didn't need him around. It's what he'd taught them from the start.

Delicious aromas seduced his senses, making his mouth water and his stomach rumble. The scent only got stronger as he neared the dining room. The table was set for a family meal, and several dishes already lined the space in the middle of the table settings. The kids took seats across from each other right before Sasha came from the kitchen carrying a large ceramic platter with a beautiful caramelized roast. He placed it at the end of the table and served perfect slices to each plate before sitting beside Ben.

Nic sank into the chair across from him and next to Lucy. He gave a rather weak laugh. "And I thought we'd be stuck with my specialties—burned grilled cheese or takeout."

"Nah. I needed something to do, and your pantry is a home cook's wet dream." The mixture of Sasha's adorable smile with that bit of verbal imagery arrowed right to Nic's heart and his cock at the same time. He took a big gulp of water, trying to cool the sudden heat in his skin, and he was glad for the flurry of activity around him, everyone passing roasted vegetables and mashed potatoes and gravy. The meal was outright divine, and why wouldn't it be? A golden angel had prepared it.

By the time dinner ended with an incredible bread pudding dessert, he was pretty much overwhelmed. Every time he'd begun to feel edged out, isolated in the presence of his own family, he'd been drawn back in. The kids were talking to him, joking with him, asking him questions. He couldn't remember the last time he'd laughed so often, the bullshit about the audit committee all but forgotten. It didn't take a wealth of analysis to figure out who'd brought him back from the outside looking in. Did Sasha see his isolation? Was he doing this deliberately?

God, his manny really was a magician, and not only with kids. He was working impossible magic on Nic, exhilarating and terrifying at the same time because now that he'd spent time with Sasha, it was more than simple physical attraction beating at Nic's resolve.

Now his heart was in danger.

Chapter Ten

Sasha

"PLEASE, don't kill me." Ben aimed his best version of puppy dog eyes at Sasha. The little brat even batted his eyelashes—long and thick like Nic's. The family resemblance was almost too much for Sasha, and he nearly decided to go easy on the kid. That, however, wouldn't do Ben any good. The fact was, if Sasha hadn't accidentally knocked over Ben's books, sending the note from the school skidding along the kitchen floor, he wouldn't have known the school had requested a meeting this morning.

Thank God McMurray Middle School was only a few miles away on the island. At least Sasha had a chance of making the meeting on time. Nic, though, had left for Seattle already, and Sasha hadn't been able to reach him other than leaving a voicemail and a text to cover the bases. That sucked big hairy balls because last time he'd meddled with the kids' school business, he'd gotten his ass handed to him. The last thing he needed was another round of admonition from Nic. No one could say Sasha never learned his lesson.

"Ben, why would you bother hiding this?" Sasha waved the half-crumpled paper between his fingers. "You had to know someone would find out."

Lucy sighed. "What do you expect from someone with one brain cell, Sasha?"

"Shut up, Lucy Loser!" Ben tried to shove Lucy, but Sasha caught him across the chest, basically clotheslining him.

"All right, stop." He guided the boy into a seat and shot a warning look at Lucy. She smirked at first. Then she rolled her eyes and leaned against the edge of the island countertop. A sulky glare settled on Ben's face, so Sasha pointed at him. "You don't get to be mad. You lied. Plain and simple. I have no idea if your uncle can get here in time for the meeting. Can you even tell me what they're gonna discuss? Are you painting bloody body parts in art class or pantsing kids in the locker rooms? Never mind. Don't answer that. I'll have to learn about your sordid activities whenever we get to the school."

Ben's eyebrows climbed upward. "*You're* going?"

"Well, you didn't give me much choice, did ya?"

Unintelligible grumbles ensued. Ignoring them, Sasha herded the kids through the chilly morning air out to the waiting car. The driver swung by Lucy's high school to drop her off first, even though it was a mile past the middle school. Then it was off to McMurray to deal with Ben's drama. Sasha waited for the surge of preteens to disperse and was a little shocked at how quickly they disappeared after the bell rang. Cockroaches in a spotlight had nothing on these kids.

The administration office was fairly peaceful, with only a few students coming in and out, but they really didn't have to wait long before being ushered in to speak to a counselor. Good news was they weren't meeting the principal or anything like that.

A grandmotherly woman with bleached hair and considerable wrinkles crossing her forehead urged them to sit. She had the friendliest face Sasha had ever seen.

"Mr. Price," she said. The second those words passed her lips, Sasha's breath seized in his chest and flutters invaded his belly. Damn his ridiculous imagination all to hell for planting the idea of sharing a name with Nic into his head. "Mr. Price?"

"Uh." He shook his head. "No. I'm Sasha Lindsey. I'm an authorized guardian in Mr. Price's absence. You should find the documentation in Ben's records."

The lady thumbed through the file in front of her until she found the paperwork. "Yes, that's it. Mr. Lindsey, then. Good to meet you. I'm Elisha Conley, Ben's counselor."

Sasha returned her handshake. "I'm curious why you requested a meeting, Ms. Conley."

Her eyes widened. "Oh my. I'm sorry if I gave the impression this was something negative." She focused on Ben. "One of your teachers mentioned your improvement, so I checked your progress. When I noted it was across the board, I spoke to your teachers, and we want to give you an opportunity—"

The door crashed open, and a bold voice boomed, "What's this about?"

Oddly, an inappropriate laugh nearly burst from Sasha. Nic stood in the doorway, breathing heavily and heartily disheveled, his hair sticking up on one side. Cute as fuck.

"Did you fly back the second you landed?" he asked.

Nic shrugged before pulling up a chair next to Sasha. "A second before landing."

"Mr. Price, I suppose?" Ms. Conley asked. Nic introduced himself briefly, and the counselor continued her spiel. When she explained that Ben could meet passing grades in his courses if he made up his coursework before the next quarter began, Sasha's heart practically swelled in his rib cage, he was so proud.

However, Ben didn't look so sure of himself.

"He'll do it," Sasha said, injecting the confidence Ben wasn't quite feeling yet. "No problem."

Ben looked at him like he'd escaped the loony bin, and all Sasha could do was chuckle. Nic finished up with the counselor as if in a near daze. He barely acknowledged Ben as the kid left to head to class.

With a grin, Sasha followed Nic out to where the car Sasha and Ben had taken waited. Nic had obviously sent his own driver away when he'd arrived at the school. Sasha slid in after Nic, who turned to face him as they headed toward the mansion.

"I can't believe it," he said. "I can't believe you got his grades up."

"You didn't think I could accomplish that, did you?" Sasha's smile melted away, and he sank back into the seat, his gaze sliding to the road passing by outside the window. Cool, elegant fingers cupped Sasha's jaw and tipped his face back to Nic.

"I didn't mean it that way, Sasha," Nic said. "I *meant* I'm in awe of you."

The tender caress of those graceful fingers along his jaw, rasping against the stubble, got his skin tingling all over his body, as if the cells of his face were connected to every last nerve ending. Nic's emerald eyes searched Sasha's. Whatever he was looking for, he must have found it, because his expression softened, a slight smile tilting the corners of his lips.

"We're here," Nic said. How long had they been sitting in the drive just staring into each other's eyes?

Nic's expression shifted and he jerked his hand back as if he'd touched a flame. Perhaps he finally remembered they were supposed to be all business. Right now, nothing felt more wrong to Sasha. He sighed and turned away, scooted out of the car, and headed inside. To his surprise, Nic followed.

"You working from home today?" he asked over his shoulder as they neared the den.

"Yes. Flying back and forth so many times didn't appeal to me. Mondays are painful enough already." He caught Sasha's left arm, his fingers curling around his biceps. Sasha took a few moments to contain the fiery sensations that always seared him at Nic's touch before he finally made eye contact.

"Thank you for being here for the kids," Nic continued.

Sasha chuckled. "Kinda in my job description, yeah?"

"Well, you've done more than your predecessors." Nic's gaze traveled to where he held Sasha, and he slowly withdrew. "I'll, uh, just be in my office."

Sasha couldn't resist watching Nic walk away, a claustrophobic longing pressing his chest. There was no doubt he'd been praised on his looks before, but Nic seemed to appreciate the things that were most important to Sasha.

ON any other weekday, he would've kept himself busy with some local sightseeing or working out. Today, he needed something more peaceful. He ended up reading, getting so lost in his book that several hours had passed before his ringing phone made him look up from the pages.

He answered it automatically.

"Could I speak to Sasha Lindsey, please?"

"Yes, you've got him." He pulled the phone away from his ear briefly to check the screen. Hmm. Unknown number.

"This is Atlas Debt Services representing Union Wholesale Lending on your outstanding mortgage balance—"

"Hold on." Sasha tossed his book down and leaned forward. "What garbage is this? The mortgage payments are current. My parents are the primary account holders, and I have emails verifying they sent the payments."

"Mr. Lindsey, according to Union's records, the last two payments were returned by the bank."

The man droned on, but a loud ringing in Sasha's ears drowned the guy out. His chest constricted until his breath came in short bursts, and his head spun. This was too much. He couldn't deal with this right now. Without warning, he hung up on the debt collector and tossed his phone on the coffee table. He sank into the sofa with his head tilted back, his temples throbbing.

There was no doubt in his mind that Robert and Lena Lindsey had sent the payment and then spent the money before it cleared their bank. His parents were probably cavorting without a care on a cruise somewhere or on an epic Monte Carlo cash-burning blowout. They didn't give a damn about saddling him with two months of payments plus whatever inflated fees the mortgage company added. It would take all the money Percy had paid him, along with most of his meager savings, to get right with the bank. *Fuck.* His parents couldn't take any better care of themselves than they had him as a child, so he should have known not to sign on to the mortgage with them, even to save his childhood home. But what could he fucking do about it now? Report his parents for check fraud?

He groaned and rubbed his hands over his face.

"Everything all right?"

It took Sasha a moment to compose his expression before standing and facing Nic. "Yeah, I'm fine."

Nic watched him a moment before approaching. "You seem upset."

"It's okay. Nothing I can't handle." He forced a smile.

"Well, there's a smile," Nic said with a grin of his own. A damned sexy grin with perfectly straight, dazzlingly white teeth. Nic could be an Armani model. "I'm not used to seeing you anything less than positive."

Sasha's heart plummeted. Of course Nic would point that out. No one was interested in a guy with baggage. *Smile for the camera, Sasha. Be the life of the party, Sasha. I don't want to hear your crap, Sasha. Just stay here by yourself if you're going to brood, Sasha. It's your fault I have to cheat on you, Sasha.*

"How's work going?" he asked.

If anything, Nic's grin grew wider. "I might have nabbed a few more sales contracts today."

He had to laugh at the playful tone in Nic's words. It was the happiest he'd ever seen Nic, and it wasn't too big a surprise given how obviously Nic was invested in his business. For whatever reason, there was also a healthy dose of relief in Nic's expression.

Sasha gave in to the lure of a relaxed, gratified Nic and moved closer, only inches away. Damn, it was insanely pleasing to look up into those green eyes that hooked deep into Sasha's libido. Nic's smile slowly faded as his gaze dropped along the length of Sasha's body before lifting to land on his lips. Nothing had ever made Sasha feel sexier than the way Nic looked at him with that heat-filled gaze.

Suddenly, his chest constricted for an entirely different reason, and all his circulation shot into his cock. Nic leaned forward, his warm breath brushing right where Sasha wanted his mouth. Then those lips on his weren't a fantasy anymore. The moment they touched Sasha's, his head drifted into the clouds, all thoughts and worries scattered. Sensation was everything, the softness of Nic's lips combined with their hard pressure. He opened beneath that force, and Nic slid his tongue inside to meet Sasha's.

With a shaky sigh of relief, Sasha deepened the kiss and leaned into Nic's body. Nothing felt better than Nic's arms wrapping around him and gliding underneath his polo shirt, fingertips digging into his flesh. Nic stroked down to grip Sasha's ass while he ground his hips against Sasha's, thrusting his dick against him. He felt so damn good. Smelled like heaven, like earthy sandalwood with a hint of something spicy. God, he could fucking lick every inch of him.

The slick warmth of Nic's mouth was making Sasha crazy with desire. He tugged at Nic's button-up and reached under the gap the second it cleared Nic's slacks. Smooth skin over rippling muscle greeted his fingers, and he reveled in the sensations. It had been so long since he'd felt this connected to a man, and they were only kissing. What would it be like to belong to Nic, to have him all the way?

The needy moans coming from Nic told him it would be better than his dreams. Sasha pulled back to see Nic's face. After a moment, Nic dropped his forehead to Sasha's, leaving his hands where they were on Sasha's ass.

"You feel amazing." Nic's tone was grudging, like admitting something unwanted.

Sasha lifted a hand to stroke Nic's face. "I'm glad. I know it's not the best idea, considering our positions, but I love what you do to me."

"Me too, but this isn't—"

"It's okay. No need to explain."

With matching groans, they pulled apart. Sasha watched Nic walk away for the second time today. But now he couldn't deny the seed of hope taking root in the back of his mind. Maybe they could have something together. Maybe if they took things slowly, they could keep things separate from their work relationship, especially since Nic wasn't often around when Sasha was officially on the clock with the kids.

Even Drew hadn't affected him so much, making him forget his surroundings and surrender so completely. The singular focus Nic aimed at Sasha when they were together was a reassurance that he wouldn't be the kind of guy to stray.

An equal mix of excitement and fear swirled in his gut. Why? Because after today, he was done avoiding this attraction. Everything felt too damn good with Nic. He was going to let things happen as they might. It could be the best decision he'd ever made in his life. Something told him this choice was likely to leave him in the wreckage, charred and broken. Even so, he couldn't even begin to force himself off the ride.

Chapter Eleven

Nic

NIC had let Percy off the hook, letting him have the day to himself after making him work over the weekend—not that there'd be much to do on a Wednesday. Even without Percy's help, Nic was done with the contracts early and hardly knew what to do with himself. The numbers were phenomenal. With expenses down and contracts increased, Leighton Price would have the biggest profits since the economic downturn had first hit. Yet again, no losses, but that never mattered to his father, who saw any decrease in profit as a loss and didn't give a damn about the reason for it.

In spite of that bitter thought, his good mood persisted. It was late afternoon, and he still had much of the day left. Having personal time wasn't something that occurred often. He thought about going out or maybe finding a date, but he'd avoided that in the past. The most horrible thing would be to hook up with someone only to run into that person again at the worst possible time. Even thinking about dating had Sasha flashing across his mind once again.

He leaned back in his chair and kicked his feet up on the edge of his desk, sending a piece of paper floating to the ground. When he picked it up and turned it over, he laughed. Fucking Percy. It was a printed photo of his friend huddling with the kids, all of them smiling at the camera. On the back were the words "People usually go home after work."

Yeah, the thought of heading home felt right. He was used to getting a sick feeling in his belly when it came time to leave, and there was no putting a finger on why. Sometimes, he thought it was the feeling of being an outsider that took over when he was home. Sometimes, he thought it was the guilt of leaving unfinished work behind. Maybe it was a little of both.

Today, though, he didn't experience any of that, but rather a sense of eagerness. He called for the duty pilot and spent the next forty minutes finishing up some emails. Then, with a smile on his face, he closed up his office and headed to the helipad on the roof. Less than fifteen minutes later, he was home, tugging off his outerwear and hanging it in the coat closet. He hadn't really needed the coat. It was cold and drizzly but not fully a downpour.

Voices came from the den, drawing him in that direction. Percy must have been doing something with the kids. Nic couldn't remember the last time he'd been home this early, and often when he was home, he was in his office working remotely. When he walked into the den, it wasn't Percy hanging out with Lucy and Ben. His friend must have gone out to enjoy his day off. He wasn't sure why he'd assumed it would be Percy. On a Wednesday, Sasha would be responsible for the children. The previous nannies, though, had left the kids alone in their rooms, other than dealing with meals and helping with homework. As his gaze landed on Sasha, his pulse sped, and it slammed into him how special Sasha was, how different from the others.

Sasha's gorgeous eyes turned toward Nic. Why did he have to always get this spreading heat reaction every time Sasha looked at him? It made it hard to function, working its way through his limbs, across his cheeks, and straight into his groin. Those eyes would make a corpse tingle with awareness. The wide smile only compounded the effect.

Trying to avoid staring, Nic turned to the kids and smiled at them. "How is everyone? What's all this?"

A couple of piles of cards sat on the table, and Sasha and the kids each held some in their hands. Lucy and Ben kept their attention on their cards as if he weren't in the room with them, a spirit passing through with barely a presence, and for a moment, he thought neither would answer him.

"Ben wanted to learn to play poker," Lucy said, "but he sucks at it. So we're about to switch to a board game."

Ben snorted and flicked his cards at her. "I beat you four times."

"Out of a gazillion rounds."

They continued to bicker, but Nic's attention hooked on to the man he'd had on his mind most of the day. Several games were stacked on the sofa behind Sasha where he sat on the floor with his legs tucked under the coffee table. He tossed his cards in the center, and Lucy collected them while Ben poked through the board games, trying to pick one to play. Sasha was more at home than Nic was in his own house with his own family. Sasha was life. Nic was a ghost in the room.

A flash of discomfort struck the center of Nic's chest, and that sensation of watching through a window flowed over him. Clenching his jaw, he started to turn away, but Sasha caught him before he could make an escape.

"Hey, you're home early," Sasha said, drawing Nic's eyes to his face. He held his hand out to Nic. "Come over here and play with us."

Before Nic could think at all, he'd slid his hand into Sasha's and let the man pull him to the floor. He'd swear Sasha squeezed his hand before letting it go. When his dazed thoughts finally kicked in, he could hardly believe it. Sasha hadn't asked but directed him to play, and he'd simply followed orders. It was so unlike him, and maybe that was why Lucy and Ben kept glancing at him like they expected him to disappear any second. It didn't matter that it took a little time for them to warm up to him. Something about joining them felt good, and that observer sensation shrank to almost nothing, replaced by a warm, fuzzy feeling he rarely experienced.

Nic unbuttoned the collar and first few buttons of his shirt and folded his sleeves up over his forearms. Then he rolled his shoulders, working the tension out of them and looking up to catch Sasha's hot gaze latching on to his movements. Sasha reached across Nic's back and dug into his muscles. Fuck if those strong fingers didn't feel like heaven. Nic fought down a groan of pleasure, but a shuddering breath left his lungs before he could curb it.

"Feels like you need some massage therapy." Sasha's voice came out slightly rougher and deeper than before, making it plain he might be as affected by the contact as Nic was. He pulled Nic closer to him to lean against the sofa before he slowly slid his hand away.

"How about Sorry!?" Lucy asked.

"Meh. I could take it or leave it," Sasha answered, his eyes never leaving Nic's face. At least this insane attraction was making Nic forget all about feeling like an outsider.

"Monopoly?" Ben asked.

Sasha snorted. "Are you freaking kidding me? You wanna play that with Mr. MBA over here?" He tipped his chin toward Nic sitting next to him. "He'd wipe the floor with us."

"I doubt it." With a flip of her hair, Lucy batted her eyelashes at Nic. "We'd 'pretty please' and cry a little here and there, and he'd be eating out of our hands." It was a playful kind of remark she normally reserved for Percy or Sasha and one that showed him she remembered much from his visits when she was little. Smirking, she gave Ben a soft shove. "Except this turd over here. He's not cute enough."

Nic surprised himself with a laugh, a real one. "I don't know, Lucy. His hair's a little curly, kind of like a cherub. That could qualify as cute."

"Noooooo," Ben howled. "I'm not cute!"

"What's wrong with cute?"

Sasha's question kicked off a discussion of male versus female attributes, gender bias, and traditional roles. They ended up settling on a Harry Potter version of Clue, ordering pizza for dinner, and following up with the Trivial Pursuit Star Wars version. Nic failed miserably at both games and made sure that before the kids headed to bed, they knew the next game night would require Monopoly. At least he could kick some butt with financial matters.

The fact they'd established a regular game night blew his mind, but he couldn't imagine doing this without Sasha here. Something about the man settled him inside and pulled him into everything without any of his customary awkwardness.

He glanced at Sasha next to him, realizing the room had been silent for several minutes now that the kids were gone for the night. Sasha had his head tipped back on the seat cushion, his Adam's apple rising and falling as he swallowed. His eyes were closed. Long, thick lashes, a few shades darker than his dark blond hair, rested against the skin above his high cheekbones.

All the relaxation Nic had gained over the afternoon went out the door as Nic's body tightened with desire. He couldn't take his eyes off Sasha. Short golden stubble dusted his lower cheeks and chin. Before Nic could stop himself, he pushed up onto his knees, hovering but not touching. Sasha barely opened his eyes enough for Nic to see the bright blue of his irises, and his lips parted as if luring Nic closer.

"Tell me something," Nic said. "When we were making cookies, you looked happy."

The corners of Sasha's mouth turned down, but he didn't say anything.

Nic braced his arms on the sofa cushion along both sides of Sasha's head, caging him in, and Sasha's pupils widened, his breath speeding up.

"But you weren't happy. Why?" he asked.

Sasha moistened his lips before answering, drawing Nic's gaze to his mouth again. "I hate baking. I hate baking with kids even more. That probably sounds awful to you. To anyone really. It's like saying you hate puppies or kittens. Because who the fuck hates anything that adorable?"

Nic shrugged. "What's so bad about baking?"

"The mess. I get so damned tired of being the one to clean up after everyone, to pay for everyone, to make everything perfect."

"Why bother with it, then?"

He started to answer and then stopped. Then he started again and stopped. "God, I don't know. I fucking don't know. It makes people happy, which I do love. I don't have to like what we do to love that part of it. Maybe I have to make sure everyone's happy."

Leaning closer, Nic considered the somber expression in front of him. Sasha was rarely without a grin nearby. Whatever he was thinking about was important to him.

"What would make you feel that way?" he asked.

For the first time since Nic's initial question, Sasha broke eye contact, dropping his gaze. Again, a visible internal struggle wound him up before he relaxed enough to explain. Nic's image of him as a completely carefree and lighthearted soul dropped back down to reality. His Adonis had demons like any other man.

"My parents. They were shallow, flighty people but more fun than anyone I've ever met. Problem was, they weren't built for kids. They couldn't deal with stress. They didn't want to deal with their own problems, much less any of mine. All the fun was theirs while they left me to take care of everything else. Traveling all over the world was their thing. They zipped through their income as soon as they collected it from their various trusts. And they left me behind, mostly." His eyes closed again, and his brow furrowed. "I wasn't fun enough, wasn't happy enough, didn't have my own money."

A powerful need to take care of Sasha, to pull him away from these painful memories, drove Nic to abandon his own resolve to stay professional. What he felt was so far from professional, there weren't words for it. He brought his arms in closer, the shift bringing Sasha's eyes open again. They widened when Nic leaned in and took his lips.

The sensation was heady, consuming. He loved the way Sasha smelled, the way he moved, the taste of him. The soft, smooth skin with hard muscle underneath beckoned his hands to trace every inch of him—his chest, his biceps, his shoulders. On and on their lips danced until his chest heaved for air. Desire flared and rampaged through Nic until his cock throbbed and his balls ached for release.

"Please," Sasha begged. "Give me more. I need more."

Sasha's throaty plea broke his barriers and drove him savage in an instant. His kiss went wild, and he pressed his mouth hard against Sasha's lips, diving deep with his tongue, relishing the rasp of that golden stubble he'd admired earlier.

Nic threaded his fingers through Sasha's hair and gripped it, holding him and maneuvering him right where Nic wanted him. Sasha moaned into Nic's mouth and wrapped his arms around Nic's waist as if desperate for greater contact.

"Dammit. I need to be closer," Nic said. He broke away and pulled Sasha up to his knees before spinning him around and pushing him facedown against the cushions. Hands shaking, he unfastened Sasha's jeans, pushed his hand into his briefs, and then freed his own cock.

"Yesss," Sasha hissed while Nic admired his view of the slightly exposed top of Sasha's firm, gorgeous ass, the flesh slightly lighter than the rest of Sasha's tanned body. "Touch me."

Nic obliged, pinning one of Sasha's wrists to the sofa cushion and palming Sasha's length with the other hand. He was more than a handful, thick and cut, with moisture slicking the tip. Sasha gasped with every squeeze of Nic's grip, every caress of his thumb beneath Sasha's cockhead.

"We can't," Nic panted in Sasha's ear. "We can't fucking do this." Yet he couldn't stop grinding against Sasha's ass, couldn't stop stroking his cock, couldn't stop biting, licking, nipping along his throat, his earlobe, sucking his skin between his teeth and leaving marks all over the golden man beneath him.

"God, Nic, I'm gonna come." Sasha shuddered under the weight of Nic's body. "I'm fucking coming."

The packed muscle under him bunched, and then a guttural cry ripped from Sasha. Nic released the grip he'd kept on Sasha's wrist to cover the head of Sasha's cock, catching the thick streams of Sasha's climax. Those sounds from Sasha's throat, the sexy gyrations of the man's hips, the out-of-control gasps for breath were hotter than the fucking sun. A moment later, Nic's own release seized him by the balls in a rush of blinding sensation. His outcry matched Sasha's—long, deep, and gritty.

When his body finally relaxed, Nic opened his eyes and stared at the view. Spent, Sasha had collapsed against the cushion with his arms outstretched like an offering. The side of his face reminded Nic of an angel's, peaceful and serene and glowing. Nic was overcome by a sudden urge to bind the man's wrists and ankles and spread him open, naked and vulnerable on his bed.

Then he glanced around the den, and cold reality set in as quickly as the sweat cooled on his skin. Anyone could have walked in on them. If not the kids, then one of the house staff members who lived in the mansion. In his head, logic reigned, telling him these scenarios were unlikely possibilities. Percy was in Seattle overnight, the staff never entered the family spaces other than to clean in the mornings, and the kids were in their rooms for the night. But knowing there wasn't really anything to fear didn't do much to reduce the adrenaline rush at the risk of getting caught in a compromising situation.

Nic couldn't deny that playing games with the kids had made this the best night for them since Josie had been alive. The last thing he wanted was to jeopardize their respect for him and their slowly strengthening bonds by getting caught in such an inappropriate situation. They'd be beyond uncomfortable to catch him and Sasha like this, and he'd be the biggest failure as their guardian to allow that to happen in the only home they had left. He had to be more careful and not get lost in the moment, no matter how difficult that was when he was with Sasha.

"And that, folks, is how you stay professional," Sasha said. He lifted his head and sent Nic such a dazzling smile, he had to bite his tongue about how much of a mistake this had been. There wasn't need for such talk because that fact was a no-brainer for both of them.

Though dismal thoughts had taken over, Nic chuckled. He rose to his feet, fastened his pants, and peeled his shirt off to wipe his fingers and then wipe Sasha clean with it. When Sasha turned over to face him, Nic offered his hand and helped Sasha to his feet.

"Thanks," Sasha murmured.

Nic nodded and headed to the service cart at the side of the room, where he poured himself a glass of whiskey. "Want a—wait. What the fuck is this?"

On the corner of the cart's silver-inlaid surface sat a thin-limbed elf doll. He'd never seen elves wearing red instead of green, but there it was, lying on its side and propping its head up with its hand.

"It's an elf on the shelf."

"Shit, that's a creepy-looking elf."

"Isn't it, though? You never heard of it before?" Sasha stood next to Nic, tracing his finger along the elf's pointy hat. "It's been popular the last few years."

Of course, he wouldn't know. Christmas had always been a calculated display in his household when he was growing up. What did he know about holiday cheer, family traditions, and fun games and activities?

"Never heard of it. Is it a decoration or something?"

"Well, the elf usually comes out right after Thanksgiving, so we're a little behind, but the elf watches to see who's naughty or nice. Every night, he returns to the North Pole to report and then appears in a new spot the next day. No one is allowed to touch him."

Nic thought about the possibilities. "So, it really is a creepy as fuck elf."

"Oh, yeah. It's the most fun ever finding funny places and situations to put the elf in each day."

"Does that mean Santa doesn't do it?"

With a light shove against Nic's shoulder, Sasha smiled. "Smartass."

Nic lifted his short glass to his lips and took a sip before waving toward the bottles on the cart. "As I started to say, would you like a drink?"

"Nah. I think I should get some sleep. Tomorrow's a school day, so the kids will be up early, and Ben needs help with the last bit of his report."

There was something unbelievably domestic and comforting about discussing family activities with

Sasha. He was a tether holding Nic in orbit to Lucy and Ben, hauling him in closer and closer when he'd been drifting so far away.

It was the worst idea, though, to become so dependent on an employee he'd so recently hired, to allow him so much influence. He barely knew Sasha, but the man had been right about the kids' care thus far. The kids weren't skipping school anymore, and there were no reports of behavioral problems. They seemed happier, more motivated, and more sociable.

"Good night, Sasha."

Nic wanted nothing more than to kiss him again, and Sasha hesitated as if it were on his mind as well. Then he tipped his head in a nod, a slight smile on his face.

"Good night, Nic."

After he'd gone, Nic sank onto the sofa with a frustrated groan. Why couldn't he have met this guy some other way? *Ha.* He should know better than to have such thoughts. He would never have time for someone if the person didn't live in his home. Standing, he stared down at the sofa. He would never look at the damned thing the same way again.

This sure as fuck complicated things.

Chapter Twelve

Sasha

SASHA stretched out on his bed, arguing with himself. He wasn't usually so lazy that he couldn't jump immediately out from the covers, but a languorous mood held him short of complete wakefulness. It wasn't a mystery why he was so relaxed. Satisfying orgasms had that sort of effect on a man, and that's what last night had brought him—a delicious, full-body, heart-pounding orgasm.

Remembering Nic's hand down his jeans sent goose bumps across Sasha's arms and chest, and then he chuckled. Damn, he was an idiot. He had a crush on his new boss. What kind of glutton for punishment did he need to be to let this happen, especially after his experience with Drew?

As if he didn't have enough problems. His parents screwing him over wasn't anything new, but they couldn't have picked a worse time to remind him why he couldn't rely on anyone but himself. Thinking about how easily he could lose everything because of their carelessness threatened to plunge his mood into the blackest depths, so he headed off his wandering thoughts and tried to focus on getting the kids ready for school instead. After all, he'd managed on his own before, and he would now.

With a groan, he rolled up and swung his legs over the side of the bed. It was still so early, there was barely any light filtering through the curtains. Actually, it seemed even darker. He allowed himself another wide yawn and got up to peek out the window. The second he did, a grin spread across his face.

Frost crystallized around the edges of the glass panes, and a layer of snow covered the ground while flurries twisted and hung in the air currents outside. It was the first snow of the season, a little earlier than the weatherman had projected. His pulse raced. Maybe the snow was thick enough to play in. The kids would love this shit, especially because snow on a Thursday likely meant two extra days added to their weekend.

Laziness evaporated in the face of his exhilaration. He threw on some weather-resistant clothes, adding a few layers to stay dry and warm, shoved his feet into waterproof hiking boots, and then headed toward Lucy's and Ben's rooms.

He pounded on Lucy's door first, and she whined a little until he pushed her toward the window and made her look outside. Her energy sparked the same as Sasha's had at the sight of the snow outside. While she searched for clothes, he did the same with Ben, who wasn't as whiny, but getting him up from bed was like raising a corpse from a grave.

They'd headed outside to the massive yard overlooking the water beyond the bay windows by the time Sasha went downstairs on a mission to drag Nic out with them. He wasn't sure Nic would relax his walls enough to join in, but he would try his damnedest to get him outside.

He knocked on the door expecting to knock a few times before getting an answer, but the door swung open almost immediately. Nic was immaculately dressed, as usual, in a crisp navy blue suit, his face freshly clean-shaven, and his hair impeccably tamed. The urge to dishevel the man slammed into Sasha.

"Wow." *Come on, Sasha. Use your words like a grown-up.* "Uh, you're dressed."

The half smile Nic sent him had Sasha's stomach flipping over a few times. "Were you trying to catch me naked?"

No. Absolutely not. Because Nic answering the door naked would give Sasha an aneurysm or something. It would have to be some kind of overload to his brain functions. As it was, his deep voice suggesting such an event got blood heading straight to Sasha's nether regions in hopes of a repeat of last night.

"I'd chase you first," he said. Nic's breath hitched audibly, his hands trembling as he pushed the door open wider.

"Jesus, Sasha."

He laughed, happy that he could rattle the self-assured billionaire so easily, before reaching out to run his fingers up and down the lapels of Nic's suit. "This won't do," he told Nic, who frowned.

"What won't?"

"Have you looked outside this morning?"

Nic shook his head, so Sasha stepped into the room and guided Nic to the window with an arm around his waist. He had to fight the impulse to pull Nic closer. Instead, he drew the curtain back.

"Ah, it's snowing," Nic exclaimed. "I guess the kids will be staying home today."

Sasha nodded. "Yeah, probably. How about you? Are you staying home today?"

The strained look on Nic's face was unexpected. He was always so decisive. "I really should head to the office."

"Or—" Sasha led Nic to the massive walk-in closet. "—you could go in late or even work from the home office. You know, with the weather being unpredictable and all."

"Sasha, why are we in my closet?"

He pushed his hands under Nic's suit jacket and slid it over his shoulders and down his arms. "We're getting you naked."

Sasha was so close while he unbuttoned Nic's white shirt, he could see Nic's pupils dilate. Nic's breath brushed along Sasha's throat and cheek as he let Sasha undress him.

"What will you do after I'm naked?" Nic rumbled next to his ear.

Lifting up on his tiptoes, Sasha skated his lips against the shell of Nic's ear. "Once you're naked," he whispered back, "I'm going to dress you in proper clothes so we can play outside."

Nic drew back to watch Sasha's face. "What? Me? Go out there?"

"Yep. So we can play in the snow. The kids are already out there waiting for us."

Shaking his head, Nic backed away. "I can't go out there and play. Are you joking?"

"Not joking, and yes, you're going out there." He tugged Nic toward him again and unfasted Nic's pants. Nic gripped Sasha's wrists before he could get any further.

"Whoa. You can't talk about chasing me down and getting me naked and playing with me, not while you're undressing me." Nic's hands tightened around his wrists and pulled Sasha closer. "Not right before pushing me out in the cold, wet snow."

Sasha laughed and was instantly cut off by a hard, rough kiss that broke off entirely too quickly. "Fuck."

"Yes. That," Nic said. "Tease."

He rubbed Sasha's wrists with his thumbs before releasing him. Then he kissed Sasha again as if he couldn't resist doing it over and over. He always pulled back before Sasha could deepen the kiss, but that was probably for the best if they wanted to leave the room anytime soon.

Nic began shedding his shirt, slowly revealing more naked flesh as his fingers worked button after button. "I guess layers would be the right choice?"

"And waterproof shoes if you have any." Sasha hoped his voice didn't sound as strangled and breathless as he imagined.

"I have some hiking boots I picked up for a camping trip I never went on."

With a shrug, Sasha nodded, stalling for time to get his hormones under control. The signs of Nic's arousal, the rosy flush in his cheeks and tension in his jawline, made it hard for Sasha to speak past the tightness in his throat. "Probably not broken in, but it'll do. Meet us outside?"

No way in hell could he stand by and watch Nic's mostly innocent striptease without pouncing. He waited for Nic's answering nod and then left the house to join the kids outside. They were working on snowmen— well, Lucy was. Ben was making some kind of igloo or snow cave. The snow was perfectly fluffy without any ice crusting over it yet—at least until it rained like it was supposed to later in the evening.

Sasha had plans, though. He quickly dug out a trench and built up a short wall. Then, he stockpiled a huge mass of snowballs of various sizes and weights. No way would he let a snow day end without a snowball war. Lucy noticed what he was doing right away and began her own stockpile, but she played dirty. She was rolling sticks into her ammo and using the dirty snow that had been stomped through, mostly from around Ben's construction site.

Just as Sasha was starting to think Nic was going to ditch them, he walked down the steps and jogged over in their direction. He shouldn't have been surprised that Nic had suitable outerwear for the snow, but somehow, he was. Instead of being clueless, he wore very trim, formfitting Arc'teryx snow gear. *Hot as hell.* If Nic wasn't careful, he'd melt all the snow. Or maybe Sasha would, if the heat in his cheeks when Nic approached was anything to go by.

No way could Sasha wait longer for Nic to come to the same decision he had, that accepting their chemistry was worth whatever fallout would tear them up later. As he settled in for a snow war, he resigned himself to a different battle—to defeat Nic's reservations. Whatever barrier was holding him back from Sasha was going down today, and to hell with the consequences.

Chapter Thirteen

Nic

NERVOUS tics irritated Nic's muscles as he headed out to meet Sasha and the kids. Yes, Sasha had invited him—demanded his presence, really—but the kids always played outside on their own. He couldn't fathom them wanting the authority figure around when they were trying to have some fun.

As he got close enough for them to notice him, though, their smiles brightened. Neither of them hesitated or half ignored his company like they had before. Maybe the game night had finally earned some of the trust he'd sought the past few years. The idea alone squeezed the center of his chest until he could barely breathe.

"Uncle Nic!" Lucy leaped over her wall and threw her arms around him. The press of her cold cheek against his warm one made him laugh and jerk back.

"You're freezing."

She snickered, and then a jolt of icy cold dripped down the back of his neck. He yelped, and Lucy ran away, diving behind her wall.

"War!" she cried, lobbing a snowball straight into his chest.

"No fair," he said. "You had a head start."

"Nic," Sasha called, waving him over to his snow bunker. When he got there, Sasha tugged him down behind the wall. "We can share."

Sasha's cheeks were flushed an adorable ruddy color, and his breath puffed out in wispy clouds. He'd never been more desirable than he was at that moment.

"You want to make the snowballs or launch them?"

"I played baseball, and my aim's not rusty. You?" Sasha asked.

"I was a swimmer and a golfer. Not much use for pitching."

"Let's do some damage." The maniacal grin Sasha sent him made him laugh out loud.

A monstrous snowball took out a chunk of their defense wall, but Ben had gotten close to be able to launch something that heavy, so he was still within range as he ran back to his trench. Sasha rose just enough over the barrier to lob a snowball, nailing Ben right on his fleeing ass. Ben screamed and rubbed the butt of his jeans as he hopped over his wall.

"Worth it!" he yelled across the yard.

Sasha was like a machine, launching ball after ball with speed, force, and accuracy, while Nic formed snowballs as quickly as he could. There was no keeping up with Sasha, though. Despite his aptitude at snowball fights, he was careful not to hit the kids anywhere sensitive, though he got hit several times—once on the side of his face, getting ice in his ear. That was something Nic loved about Sasha, his willingness to give others a chance to win. He'd done the same thing last night during their board games, making sure no one felt awful about the game's outcome. Nic had never seen anyone so centered on making everyone else happy.

Fuck, that had to be exhausting.

The thought bit into Nic and wouldn't let go. He turned and studied Sasha's smiling face. Was Sasha as happy as he seemed? At first glance, he'd say yes, but the tiniest bit of tension around Sasha's eyes said he was worried about something. When he caught Nic looking at him, that tension abandoned his expression and the smile widened into something wholly genuine. The thrill of bringing that out in him sent Nic soaring on an endorphin rush.

"We're almost out of ammo," Nic said. He'd been hit multiple times too, but mostly because he was more focused on forming the balls than on his surroundings. Luckily, his outerwear was high-quality and waterproof, keeping most of him dry.

"Yeah, I'm about ready to call a peace treaty and move on to the next competition."

"What's that?"

But Sasha was already over the wall and waving the kids in. Nic joined them, and Lucy hit him with one last snowball, complaining about not hitting Nic enough times.

"What the heck, Lucy? Are you trying to get back at me for something?"

"I have ice down the back of my pants, right into my butt crack. I'm getting back at you for teaming up with Sasha."

"Hey, no one said you couldn't team up with Ben," Sasha pointed out.

"What? Why didn't we think of that?" Ben asked. "Wait. Why'd we stop? I'm not frozen yet."

"We're having a contest now. Everyone gets to build a snowman or snowperson or whatever. Best one gets a prize." Sasha turned to Nic. "What should they get?"

"And who's judging?" Lucy puffed her breath out as she pretended to smoke.

"You automatically lose if you keep doing that," Nic said. She grinned at him and threw her imaginary cigarette on the snow and pretended to grind it out. "How about a day off for whoever wins, school or work?"

Cheers abounded, and the easy normalcy of the moment hit Nic all at once, nearly choking him up. Once he'd gotten outside, there'd been no awkward moments. He wasn't an outsider here but a welcome family member playing with loved ones. The kids hadn't looked at him with fake smiles or blank expressions, waiting patiently for him to go away.

"I'll judge," he told them. He watched as they raced to build their snowmen. Lucy went literal with her design, opting for tradition. Ben? Who the hell knew what Ben was making? It looked like a penis between a pair of balls, but Nic didn't want to say it out loud in case he'd misinterpreted the snow sculpture.

He couldn't tell what Sasha's was yet. It was a large, wide lump with two smaller oblong lumps pressed against the big lump's side. As the time passed and more of the sculpture became clear, Nic smiled. It was a dog, an incredibly lifelike dog. Sasha began shading using the dirt he'd dug down to, and he pressed dark stones in for the eyes and a chunkier one for the nose. The dog was a husky, judging by the markings.

Most of their figures were complete when Lucy's phone rang. She answered and within a few minutes, she'd arranged for her and Ben to go sledding with her friend's family while the snow was still thick. Nic ended up giving the prize to all of them, and before he was ready to abandon the ever-evasive family time, the kids were gone, packed away in the minivan with several sleds and tubes. Sasha stood close enough to touch arms as they watched the van pull carefully down the drive.

They walked side by side back to the front of the house. When they reached the first step, Sasha slid on the newly formed ice. Nic just caught him but not in time to keep Sasha from clipping himself on one of the steps.

"Ow, ow, fuck!" Sasha covered the bleeding scrape above his right eyebrow with a hand. "Great. Now I feel like an idiot."

Nic chuckled as he helped Sasha get to his feet. "Why?"

"I'm supposed to be an athletic, agile man with a great sense of balance."

Nic guided Sasha to the first-floor guest bathroom where a first aid kit was stored before he lost his mind, forgetting all about his resolve to stay professional. "Well, maybe it's better if I keep you on your back, then."

Sasha had been leaning against the sink counter at first, but after Nic's comment, he lowered the toilet seat cover and sank down to sit on it. His silence was unnerving.

"I'm sorry, I—"

"Maybe you should," Sasha said as Nic crouched in front of him to clean the blood from the scrape above his eye. "Keep me on my back, I mean."

Nic didn't answer but continued caring for the wound. He cleaned it with an antiseptic wipe, wincing at Sasha's hiss at the contact, and pressed a long, slender bandage across the cut. With their faces very close, Nic's eyes met Sasha's for a long while before he spoke again.

"I don't think I've ever had this much fun," Nic murmured, afraid to break the connection growing between them.

Sasha's lips quirked up at the corners. "I'm glad it was fun. I had fun too. You've never played in the snow?"

"That obvious, huh?" Nic's laugh was halfhearted. "I've gone skiing before. Nothing else, though."

"I liked that igloo Ben had going on before the snowball fight. If there was enough snow, it could be pretty amazing." Sasha leaned even closer. "Just wondering what the hell he made for the snowman competition."

Nic huffed out a chuckle. "I had some ideas, but they weren't fit for mixed company."

"Penis and balls, I take it?" Sasha grinned widely. "You don't even need to answer. You're blushing."

Yes, he was. The warmth of it wasn't only in his cheeks but spreading all over his body as his attraction to Sasha sank him in desires he couldn't deny anymore.

"It was a little family of snow people he was making, an adult and two kids. I think the penis was you, Nic." He laughed. "Don't tell Ben I thought he and Lucy looked like balls, though."

There was no one on the planet cuter and sweeter than a teasing, laughing Sasha. *Fuck it.* Sasha clearly wanted this too. Nic swooped in and took Sasha's mouth, pushing his tongue inside to glide against Sasha's. There was nothing holding him back anymore.

"You okay?" he asked, panting against Sasha's mouth. "No headache or anything?"

Sasha shook his head slightly, unable to answer, his pupils blown and his breath rushing in and out. He unzipped Nic's coat and pushed it off him, his movements frantic, impatient. Just as quickly, he whipped off his Carhartt and peeled off two more layers before revealing that golden, masculine chest Nic loved so much.

"Goddamn, Sasha." Nic ran his hand all over the soft skin and hard muscles before finding Sasha's nipples and playing with them, circling, tweaking, and lightly tugging before he tongued and sucked on them one by one, drawing heady, deep moans from Sasha.

He leaped to his feet, pulling off his two shirt layers, kicking off his shoes, and dragging his pants down his legs until he was naked for the first time in front of Sasha, who utterly devoured him with his eyes.

"I love the way you look at me," Nic said.

"I love looking at you." Sasha smiled a real smile, the kind that took over his whole face. "Get me naked, Nic."

Sasha lifted up while Nic drew his jeans and briefs down. Holy fuck, Sasha was perfectly formed, like he'd been set from a precise mold. He'd barely cleared the clothing from Sasha's legs before he knelt in front of him and ducked his head to take Sasha into his mouth and blow his mind.

Too bad Sasha bent for a kiss at the same time. Their skulls collided enough to jar Nic, so he couldn't imagine how much it had to hurt Sasha's already wounded head.

"Oh fuck," Sasha groaned, his voice tight with pain. "It was all going well until that last second. Good thing I was sitting."

"Sorry." Still kneeling, Nic lifted his hand to run it through Sasha's hair. "How is it? Okay?"

Sasha winced but nodded and then went for Nic's lips again, sliding his arms over Nic's shoulders to wrap around him. The kiss barely deepened before Sasha pulled away suddenly and braced his elbows on his knees. He cradled his head in his hands.

"Nope. Not okay enough," Nic said.

"Might be feeling a little sick," Sasha mumbled before peeking up at him.

He leaned his head against Sasha's shoulder, trying to get his breathing under control. "You should lie down. I'll call for a doctor to check on you." Then, ignoring Sasha's muttered protest, he cupped Sasha's jaw. "I like you, Sasha. So much," he said. "I didn't want to. We're not in the best situation, but—"

"I like you, too, Nic, and I know it's not the best circumstances. I want this too much to care, though."

"Yeah?" He waited for Sasha's nod. "Okay, but we need to keep it to ourselves. You okay with that? The kids can't find out, at least not for a while. I don't want them to get confused about anything."

"It's all right," he said. "I can live with that."

That expression had reappeared on Sasha's face, the one with the tension all around his eyes while a fake smile stretched across his face. Nic would love to replace it with something real, but it wasn't something he could do for Sasha in this case. It didn't matter how strong their attraction. The fact was, Sasha was his employee, and he'd never seen workplace relationships succeed.

Who the fuck was he kidding? He'd never seen any relationship work out. Still, he was going to enjoy every second with Sasha while their time together lasted because it wouldn't be long before whatever was between them fizzled out.

Chapter Fourteen

Sasha

AS Sasha leaned into the open fridge in search of milk, a hand slid up his spine to grip the top of his shoulder and hook him back against hips that moved suggestively. He laughed and pushed back into them.

"Careful," he said, hearing the smile in his own voice.

"What?" Nic said. "Like the kids would be awake anywhere near this early on a Saturday."

It had been a few days since the first wild hookup he'd had with Nic after the board games, but there hadn't been any efforts to *break the seal*, so to speak. His knock on the head hadn't helped, but he'd been all good after a few hours. What they had been doing was a lot of sneaky fooling around and making out in darkened corners, the alarms in the back of his mind that warned him of trouble ahead diminishing more and more each day. Nothing felt better than leaving his anxiety behind and permitting himself the joy of touching Nic and being touched. He couldn't believe he'd ever thought of Nic as an iceman.

Last night in the laundry room still played on repeat in the back of his mind. He relived the tight grip of Nic's hand in his hair, guiding Sasha's head up and down while Nic fucked his mouth. Nic had been the perfect size, longer than Sasha, though not quite as thick. It had been late at night with no one around to walk in on them unexpectedly, and they'd locked the door.

Still, they needed to be careful. It wouldn't take much of a slipup for them to crash and burn.

Nic's surprised laugh nabbed Sasha's attention. "What the hell?" Nic pointed to the middle of the island.

"Well, I guess the elf is watching the kitchen today." He shrugged, eyeing the scrawny elf doll lying flat on its back on top of a small pile of white powder.

"The elf on the shelf is part of a Colombian cartel?" Nic asked.

"Pretty sure that's flour." Then Sasha rolled his eyes. "And please, don't tell me you don't know about making snow angels."

"What if I didn't?"

"I'd teach you." Sasha leaned over the counter to kiss Nic on the lips. "I'm making french toast. Interested?"

"Damn, that sounds good."

"Have a seat." Sasha set the milk on the counter and grabbed the eggs, cinnamon, and vanilla.

"Hmm." The low rumble of Nic's voice always stirred up Sasha's arousal. "I thought you weren't into baking."

He grinned. "This doesn't qualify in my book. I don't mind cooking or even baking on my own. I clean as I go." He whisked the ingredients together while the griddle heated. "There's a trick I like to use with these babies—aside from using thick bread anyway. Add a little bit of sweetened condensed milk in place of part of the milk, like so."

Nic's gaze followed Sasha's movements, his head tilted to one side. As usual, Sasha loved the way Nic looked at him. There was always a slight edge of surprise there, as if he could hardly believe his eyes. It was flattering, but Sasha was the real lucky one. Where would he ever find another man like Nic?

Though he often seemed strict, aloof, and cold, Nic appeared to want more connection to people around him, and Sasha was already addicted to the way Nic positioned and controlled his body, taking pleasure from it without hesitation.

"Your parents teach you how to cook?"

"Pffft. That would require an ounce or two of responsibility, and one thing about my parents is, they run as far and fast as possible from anything resembling that." He filled a mug with coffee for Nic, not bothering with the cream and sugar that Nic always eschewed. "Would you believe I taught myself by watching cooking shows? Oh, and there's always the internet."

"Probably learned more that way. Only thing I learned from my parents was how to be a high-class brand of asshole and how to devour the organs of my enemies."

"Right." Sasha laughed. "Except you're not one and you haven't."

"Not that you've seen yet," Nic said gruffly. "Give it time. You see your parents often?"

"Hah. Maybe once every year or two. If I want to see them, I have to track them down and fly out wherever they are. I hate to say this, but sometimes I want to forget having to take care of them and just move on with my own life."

Nic frowned. "Christ, Sasha." He was quiet for a few minutes while Sasha loaded a plate with french toast, bacon, and eggs. "I'm sorry."

"What? Why?"

He shook his head. "You shouldn't have to take care of your parents. You're way too damn young for that."

"You know, it's not so much the management of their affairs. I just can't fucking afford to pay their bills anymore. The mortgage is killing me, and they forget more often than not."

"Shit. Why not stop paying? Maybe they'll learn to stop *forgetting*."

"It's not that easy. They won't learn. They'll give up what we have because it's easier to let it go than deal with the work of keeping things. And worse, my name's on the mortgage, so I'd only be fucking myself." He laughed, trying not to sound too bitter. Truth was, he might be fucked either way after his parents' latest delinquency. "I'd only consider it to save my precious baby—my truck, I mean. Sometimes, I think I'm linked to it so if I died, my soul would be stuck in there like *Christine* or something."

"Kinda hard to kiss you like that." A smile lightened Nic's features. "I take it you can't talk to your parents about what they're doing to you."

"Hell no. Problems make them run even more than responsibilities. Anytime I argued with them, needed help, or got in any of my angsty teen moods, they'd leave or send me away. Mostly leave, though.

Sometimes for a few hours and sometimes for a few weeks. Depended on their mood and how likely my problems were bound to last."

Sasha sat on the stool next to Nic, pushing his food around the plate more than eating it. He hadn't confided all this crap to anyone in years, and he wasn't sure how to feel about it after only knowing Nic for a few weeks.

Nic reached over and rubbed the back of Sasha's neck. "I wish I hadn't killed your mood with all my nosy questions." His words were subdued, barely a whisper.

He hadn't been trying to make Nic feel bad, and he liked that Nic cared enough to ask about his life, something more than he ever expected from the man. It was getting harder and harder to remember Nic was his employer. They certainly behaved more like partners than anything.

"Meh. You haven't killed it. Besides, I'm fairly sure if you move your hand south and start rubbing there, you can improve it further."

"You still have jokes. My work here is done."

Sasha couldn't keep the grin off his face as he rose and began cleaning up. "You think those kids will sleep all day?"

"A couple more hours anyway," Nic answered. "You can leave all that. I hire people to do the cleaning for us."

Sasha set the dishes next to the sink and approached the center island, where Nic sat finishing his coffee, wearing soft-looking gray flannel sleep pants and a plain white T-shirt that clung to the defined muscles underneath. He was reading the news feed on his phone, and Sasha couldn't stop ogling the shape of his wide pecs and thick biceps, the sharp angles of his face that gave him an often harsh aspect, the stretch of fabric over hard thighs, the dark hair sleep-tousled and making him fantasize about Nic in a bed. Fuck. He wanted that body over him, pushing him down into the mattress, and it wasn't fair they still hadn't been fully skin to skin yet.

When Nic glanced up from his screen, the slow smile spreading on his face said he had some idea where Sasha's mind had gone. He'd started to stand when the kitchen door swung open and Lucy came in. She stared at Sasha and then Nic and then back again.

"Well, you guys are early."

Sasha cleared his throat. "I think that's our line."

She laughed. "I left my window open last night by accident. There was too much light, and it was so cold, I couldn't sleep anymore. Sorry to ruin your preconceptions about lazy teens."

"It's almost winter," Nic said. "Were you trying to go into hibernation or something?"

"Har-har. You've been around Sasha too much lately."

He exchanged a look with Nic as Lucy searched the fridge for the milk. Nic's jaw had tightened, his lips forming a thin line. Was Nic thinking they had been too noticeable the past few days with so much time together? He hoped not, because it wasn't enough time and definitely not enough privacy. How could anyone find sneaking around fun or exciting? It was more like an exercise in torture.

"I could make you some french toast since you missed the first batch."

"No thanks. I'm in a Cocoa Pebbles mood."

He chuckled as he watched her stir until each cereal piece was coated with milk. "We're like twins with that."

"What?" she asked, looking up from her bowl.

"Well, it's all about getting enough flavor in the milk until it tastes like liquid chocolate."

"Sh," she whispered harshly, nodding toward where Nic sat with a bemused smile replacing the earlier tension. "The adults aren't supposed to know the secret."

He pulled one of her blond curls and let it spring back. "Gotcha. Keep it between us, then."

She hip-checked Nic and waved a peace sign at the elf on the center island counter before she walked out the door juggling her bowl, an oversized mug of coffee, and an apple.

Crap. He truly loved Lucy, but she'd effectively crushed any plans to get that skin to skin with Nic that he wanted so badly. The thwarted passion building up all week long had taken a toll. How would he feel in another week? A month? He was not made for this at all. He needed to be open and free with his relationships, which was why he was fully out as it was. Was this even a relationship? Neither of them had spoken a word to define what was going on between them.

Part of him wanted to get back where they were before they'd ever touched each other. But now it was too late. After having a taste of him, he needed Nic inside him, getting the full effect of his desire, before he could let their affair end.

Had he ever wanted a man this much? Not even his longest relationship, the one with Drew, had fired him up like this, charged him with a constant buzzing energy while he anticipated the next time he'd see Nic, smell him, hear him, feel him.

"I hate this, but I got an important message, so I have to go work right now," Nic said, dragging Sasha's attention back from his thoughts. "You have plans today?"

He considered it. It might do him good to get away and have some male contact other than Nic for a while. But that buzzing energy held him back. What if he missed an opportunity with Nic because he went out? "Nothing, really. Going to run, of course."

"You're a beast. It has to be twenty degrees outside."

His smile was real enough, but inside, restlessness whipped at his levity. "Weather be damned. I don't like to be cooped up. I have no idea how you can sit in an office for hours at a time without going insane."

"So maybe I'm already insane." Nic strode over until he stood in front of Sasha, towering over him, inching forward until their chests touched. He nuzzled Sasha's cheek and then grazed his lips down to the side of Sasha's neck. A burst of Christmas music from somewhere in the house made Nic freeze, reminding both of them they weren't alone. "Fuck my life."

"Yeah. Fuck." With regret, he turned away from Nic. "I do have a little personal business to take care of, but I'll probably hang out with the kids."

Nic caught his arm before he could get out the door. "Hey, you know you don't have to. You're not working today."

"I know, but I like them. They're fun and easy to be with."

"Does that mean I'm not?"

Sasha looked over his shoulder at Nic's guarded expression. "No, it doesn't mean that. It means they're here, I'm here, and you're busy. That's all. Would you rather I leave?"

He held his breath as he waited for Nic's answer. If he said yes, it might stab him right through his pulpy little heart because it meant Nic wanted him in a tiny box with nothing but strict personal boundaries for walls.

"No," Nic answered, rubbing his arm before releasing him. "I think I'd go nuts wondering where you were and who you were with."

Disbelief sank in. That smacked of possessiveness if he'd ever heard it. Fuck if that didn't sound amazing and delicious. Yeah, most empowered people might call it a warning sign of controlling, abusive behavior, but Sasha couldn't help his feelings. There was a sweet spot where emotional greed behind those demanding behaviors struck a balance with trust in a partner.

He'd always been weak about possessive men, at least on the inside. No, he'd never let a man control his life, but it filled a need. It meant he was wanted more than as a passing interest, wanted enough to consume another man's thoughts. Drew had never cared who he spent time with or even how much time he was away from home. Maybe that should have told Sasha something about how much Drew had cared for him—not at all, as it'd turned out.

Before the silence stretched long enough to be awkward, Sasha said, "Don't spend too long on the phone sex. We know that's what you do in there during those long office hours at home."

Nic laughed and wrapped him in a tight hug from behind that was much too quick for his satisfaction. It was the kind of hug that used the whole body, a real I-want-to-touch-every-part-of-you kind of hug. Then he went out the door ahead of Sasha.

When Sasha got to his room, he threw himself across the bed on his belly and pulled his laptop from the side table. He should have known nothing good ever came from checking his email. The collector for the mortgage company was practically spamming his email since he'd stopped taking their phone calls.

He was lucky he'd received his first monthly deposit of his salary. He was unlucky that the damned mortgage wiped him out the rest of the way when added to his student loans, truck payment, and credit card payments. He should never have gone so far into debt when he'd been with Drew. It'd only made his financial position more precarious.

It was a good thing he'd decided to stay home over going out this weekend. He'd have to live like a pauper the next two weeks if he wanted to make his truck payment at the end of the month. Nothing could make him risk losing his precious Silverado, the only nice thing he'd ever done for himself. He blew out a lungful of air and rolled onto his back. If this shit kept up, he'd be old and gray by the time he hit the age of thirty.

With a quite impressive dose of unease, he acknowledged that if he'd been in any other job, this month would have put him on the street. This job offered him more than average for a nanny salary, paying him four thousand a month for minimal hours, giving him free weekends, and including room and board without any pay deductions. He didn't have to clean or cook either.

It made fucking around with Nic even more hazardous to his health, both mental and financial. He had no room to mess this up. The kids were too important and so was his stability. Lucy and Ben were doing so much better than when he'd first arrived. They'd been so closed off, angry, defensive, isolated. Now, they'd stopped hiding in their rooms, stopped leaving school in the middle of the day, and Ben had stopped fighting with other kids.

It probably wasn't all him. Nic was around much more lately, and that had a noticeable effect, at least from a newcomer's perspective. The kids seemed to soak up Nic's attention. He wasn't sure why he'd been so worried about it all when Nic had first returned, though Lucy had given him a different idea of what to expect from Nic.

Sasha sent Percy a quick text letting him know he'd be home with the kids today if Percy needed the day out of the house. Then he rolled back to his laptop and worked what magic he could to shift money around and pay what needed paying and shrink what payments he could shrink. By the time he was done, his head ached, throbbing in time with his pulse. He popped a few pills, downed a glass of water, and decided to skip out on his run. It could relax him, but it would more likely elevate his blood pressure. Instead, he darkened the room as much as possible, shucked his sweatpants, and crept under the covers to sleep his pain away.

It somewhat worked in that the pain had backed off to some extent several hours later, but his sleep had been sporadic, a hazy in and out of semiconsciousness while his worries battered him. Keeping it all inside wasn't good, but who the fuck was he going to talk to? He'd said more than enough about his troubles to Nic already, and the last thing he could tolerate was looking like some whiny bitch to him. Running a huge multinational corporation had to be stressful enough without one of his employees dumping personal problems on him. The kids were out of the question. He was supposed to care for them, not the other way around.

Checking his watch, Sasha groaned. It was well into the afternoon, closer to dinnertime, and he'd missed lunch. He couldn't hear any sounds in the house, downstairs or upstairs. Knowing Nic, he was probably still closed up in his office, but what were the kids doing today?

He slid out of bed, went through a bevy of stretches, hit the shower and shave routine, and jogged down the steps, trying to activate his defunct well of energy. Following voices and more Christmas music, he found Lucy and Ben on opposing sofas, pointedly ignoring each other while they worked on homework. Well, Lucy was doing homework while Ben was on his phone. It was always so obvious from their body language when they'd fought recently.

"I guess you two do need a sitter."

Ben threw his arms wide, setting his phone aside. "Nu-uh. Are you freaking kidding me?"

He ruffled Ben's hair, the kid protesting as he did. "What? Too old to have another man touch your hair? How do you get through a haircut? Speaking of haircuts, you need one badly."

Lucy snorted, trying to suppress her laughter.

"Oh, that's attractive." Ben shot visual daggers in Lucy's direction. "Do it again so I can record it and send it to Damian." He stretched out the name into an almost musical taunt.

A pillow sailed over the table and hit Sasha in the face. "Ouch."

"Oops. Sorry, Sasha," Lucy yelped.

He tossed the pillow back. "You caught me with the button on there." He rubbed his cheek, hoping it didn't leave a mark. "Also, your aim stinks. I think we should work on that."

"How?"

He waved his hand. "Who cares? Paintball maybe? I'm more interested in hearing about Damian." He duplicated the taunting notes Ben had made earlier.

"Never mind." Her blush and dodgy eye contact said a lot about who the guy was to her.

"Ah, a boyfriend? It has to be, or you want him to be."

"Not a boyfriend," she explained, "but he asked me to the holiday dance. I really like him, Sasha."

He shrugged, and Ben made kissing sounds, which Lucy ignored. "So go with him. What's the problem?"

"Just go? Whatever. Uncle Nic would never let me. I've never been to a dance with a boy, only my girlfriends when I was Ben's age."

"Sheesh. Make yourself sound so old there, Luce," Ben said.

Sasha sat back in his seat. "Okay, how about this? We'll work on him together, get him to cave a bit. There's gotta be a first time, right? So why not now?"

Her eyebrows lifted. "Really?"

"Sure, let's do it. Solidarity and all that." He nudged Ben with an elbow. "You too."

Ben rubbed his hands over his head. "Well, I guess, but only if you guys help get him to go to the Christmas musical next week."

"Hey, you didn't tell me about it." He gave Ben a mock glare. "You don't want me there?"

"Well, I wouldn't complain, but I've been doing this every year, and Uncle Nic never comes. It's the last year before I go to high school. There won't be another one."

"Ah, I get it. Of course, I'll see what I can do. Maybe we can squeeze both out of him."

"How, though?" Lucy asked.

He stretched his arms up and then folded them behind his head. "I'm not sure yet. Getting him in a holiday spirit might help."

"Yeah, right. He doesn't even decorate the house." The slump of Ben's shoulders showed how firmly he lacked hope.

"He baked Christmas cookies with us," Sasha pointed out. "Let's do a holiday movie night tonight. We can catch him late so he can't use work as an excuse."

"Oh, he can *always* use work as an excuse," Lucy said.

Jumping up from the couch, Ben headed toward the hallway. "I'm game. I'll go pick out some movies and start the popcorn machine."

Sasha pursed his lips and looked at Lucy. "Where's he going?"

"There's a home theater near the back of the house, not far from Percy's room." She looked up from her textbook. "You never did get a full tour, did you?"

"Not really." He laughed. "Christmas break will be here before you know it. You ready for Christmas?"

"Not even." She gave up on the book, closing it and setting her work aside. "We haven't had a chance to go Christmas shopping yet. We usually go right after Thanksgiving, but Uncle Nic was gone for weeks, and then we got in trouble the first weekend he was back."

"Okay, let's fix that too, then." He stood, about to talk to Vicki, the family's personal chef, about making something special for dinner. "We can soften him up tonight, get him to go shopping tomorrow, and that's when we'll work on the dance and Ben's musical. Sound good?"

Her smile lit up her face. "Yes, yes, yes! And before I forget, thank you, Sasha, for the zoo day. My team won the debate on Friday, and the notes I got from the tours helped a ton."

Sasha stepped over the table to lean down and give Lucy a hug. "You have no idea how happy that makes me."

A couple of hours later, they had dinner, but Nic didn't join them, opting to have dinner brought to his office. Disappointing, yes, but Sasha wasn't ready to give up the day, and he didn't let the kids lapse into negativity either. Right as the sky grew dark, he poked his head in Nic's office.

"Who are you?" Sasha said.

Nic seemed confused at first and then laughed. "Have I been locked away so long that you'd forget my face?"

"Too long to bear," he answered, moving the rest of the way into the room. Nic stood and came around the desk, hesitating only a moment before grabbing Sasha's hips and pulling him in. The kiss that followed scorched down his spine in a flash. Then Nic's hand traveled down to cup Sasha's cock, making him growl with pleasure.

"Fuck, Nic." He wanted to pretend nothing else existed at that moment, but unfortunately, he'd made some commitments to the kids. "As much as I'd love to pretend I'm a hot new secretary you're interviewing—"

"You're hired, now bend over the damned desk, dammit." Nic squeezed Sasha's ass, running a hand between his legs from behind.

Sasha groaned. "God, why did I propose a movie night?"

"Movie night?" Nic's hands returned to Sasha's hips, and he broke his lips away from the column of Sasha's throat.

"Yeah. Me, you, and the kids with some popcorn and Christmas movies. Interested?"

Stunned. That was the only way to describe how Nic looked for the span of three seconds. Then he composed himself and cleared his throat. "Uh, sure. I'm done in here. Are we in the den or the theater?"

"Theater because the kids outvoted me. Plus, I've never seen, much less been in, a home theater in my life."

"All right." The way he stroked Sasha's face made Sasha quiver all the way to his feet. "Let's fix that right now."

Nic took Sasha's hand and led him to the other side of the first floor. It was, indeed, not far from Percy's suite, but the kids said the walls were soundproofed. Percy was probably out anyway, enjoying the rare free time.

Sasha hadn't seen Lucy and Ben so excited since the zoo day. Even then, this night might have been a notch higher in level. The room sloped down, creating a stadium feel with lots of leg room between the three rows of six seats. Each wide, plush, dark leather seat reclined and had a footrest and drink holders. It truly imitated a miniature version of a luxury theater. There was even a minibar on the side of the room.

"Holy shit," Sasha breathed. "I'll get so spoiled here."

Nic traced his finger softly across the back of Sasha's hand before releasing him to gather popcorn from the machine—they had a freaking full-sized popper!—and some drinks. Sasha had assumed the kids would choose to sit on either side of Nic, but they didn't, opting for the bottom row centered in front of Nic's seat in the back row. Sasha sat at his right. They used a rather complex remote to dim the lights and control the digital components, and then the movies started.

Sasha barely noticed the selection of movies and which one ended up playing because all he could focus on was the warmth of Nic's hand. Not long after the lights dimmed, bathing them in darkness, Nic lowered his hand to Sasha's upper thigh, sliding up and down, nudging Sasha's legs apart. The man drove him utterly crazy with his nails dragging along the inner seam of Sasha's jeans. If the kids hadn't been in the room, no doubt that hand would have been inside those jeans. Not that the kids would notice. Those two were talking all the way through the movie—oh right, *A Christmas Story*—heckling the funniest parts and wolf whistling at each appearance of the leg lamp. With them on the other side of the theater and Sasha sitting low in the deep seat, there was no way for them to see anything beyond the middle row of seats anyway.

Keeping his breath even was nearly an exercise in futility. His chest trembled with the effort. It wasn't long before Sasha started rocking his hips up, seeking Nic's hand. His own fingers dug deep into the arms of the reclining seat while Nic studiously avoided Sasha's attempts at relief.

Slowly, Nic leaned over until his lips touched the shell of Sasha's ear. "Don't you make a fucking sound."

A small burst of an exhale escaped before he could stop it, and Nic pinched the inside of Sasha's thigh in warning. *Fucking hell!* His body ignited, every single goddamn cell of it. Nic resumed teasing Sasha through his jeans, increasing the pressure closer to his groin but never touching anything but his thighs. Friction made the contact even hotter, and tremors shook him to his bones as he fought back his reactions.

After a torturous hour and a half kept on the edge, the movie came to an end, but Sasha didn't trust his legs to stand. Luckily, Nic didn't bring the lights all the way up.

"I'm glad we did this," Nic said to Lucy and Ben. He stood and walked with them to the door, subtly ushering them.

"We kind of had an ulterior motive," Lucy said. As she tried to lean around Nic, he put his arm around her shoulders to maneuver her out. Ben was outside, having already said good night to Sasha from the end of the seat row.

"Yeah? What's that?" Nic asked.

"We hoped you'd take us Christmas shopping tomorrow," she said. Sasha could barely see it, but Lucy had her best pleading face on.

"Sure. Let's do it." Nic didn't sound nor look enthusiastic about it but did sound impatient. At least to Sasha's ears. All Lucy heard was a yes, and she ran with it, throwing her arms around Nic and squealing in his ear.

"Thanks, Uncle Nic." She nearly fled the room and then caught herself before the door closed. "Good night, Sasha!"

With that, they were alone again. Nic's efforts to protect Sasha from the embarrassment of discovery and to allow Sasha recovery time made him melt inside. He slumped lower in his seat, body still thrumming with need.

The click of the lock seemed amplified in the silence. Sasha looked up in time to watch Nic stalk down the slope and along the rear row of seats to where he sat and crouched in front of him. Faster than Sasha could finish taking a deep breath, Nic's hand was down the front of Sasha's jeans, caressing his cock up and down in a deliciously tight grip, his thumb rubbing just beneath the head.

"Fuck, Nic," he gasped.

As Nic sped up the pace, Sasha couldn't help himself. His hand clamped over Nic's wrist while he ground his hips against each stroke. His head pushed deeply into the headrest. He clenched his jaw as his body locked up with the most intense orgasm he'd ever had. And it just kept fucking going on and on. When it finally let him go and he sagged into the seat, tears burned Sasha's eyes, so he kept them firmly closed until he could come back from whatever crazy headspace he'd gone to. As he settled, Nic gently cleaned him with a handkerchief and then continued to softly stroke his thigh.

"I think you might have ended me." Shit. Even his voice was gone, more of a rusty grating sound than anything.

"God, that sounds fucking sexy, Sasha. Say something. Anything." Nic stood, and Sasha roused enough to watch him unbuckle his belt and unfasten his black trousers, his eyes fixed on Sasha's face as he loomed over him.

"Nic—"

In a heartbeat, Nic pressed his thumb between Sasha's lips. "Suck it."

As if he'd needed the order. It'd been his first urge, so he obeyed, tracing the flesh with his tongue as he did.

"Then you're going to suck this." Nic pushed his trousers down and pulled out his cock, already swollen and flushed and damp at the head. Releasing Nic's thumb, he licked Nic from root to tip before taking him in his mouth while he held Nic's balls in his palm, rolling and caressing them. He gave everything he could, licking, sucking, bottoming out and closing around the head as he swallowed. Reaching farther behind Nic's sac with his fingertip, he traced Nic's hole, applying light pressure as he worked.

He would have loved to drag this out and torture Nic as much as he'd been tortured, but Nic wasn't a patient sort of man. He was already directing Sasha's mouth, not permitting any lapse in rhythm. Without warning, Nic climaxed, holding Sasha in place until every spasm was complete.

They were both panting like marathon runners, and Nic sank to his knees on the floor in front of Sasha's seat. He laid his head on Sasha's quivering belly and groaned.

"Maybe we should just sleep in here," Nic said. "It's too much effort to move."

Sasha laughed, petting Nic's dark, slightly sweat-dampened hair. "Call Percy next door. He's strong and can carry us."

"Ugh, nasty. If that's not motivation to move, I don't know what is." He stood, pulling Sasha up with him, and they began fixing their clothes. "That was amazing, but I think in my haste to send the kiddos off to bed, I might have volunteered for something on the opposite spectrum."

"Would Christmas shopping be so bad?"

He gave Sasha a look that clearly stated *you must be nuts*.

"Oh. That bad, huh? You need a buffer? I could go with you."

Nic looked surprised again. "Are you sure? It's another day off for you."

"More than sure. I want to go right now."

Sasha followed Nic out, but Nic kept leading the way to the front staircase of the house instead of heading alone toward his master suite. When they stopped at the bottom of the stairs, Nic spun Sasha toward him and kissed him softly on the lips before drawing back.

"I question your judgment. It's Christmas shopping at the mall. Everyone and their twin will be there."

Sasha just smiled and waved as he trudged up the stairs, his legs not the steadiest yet. "Sweet dreams, Nic."

"Have a good night, Sasha."

No doubt about that. He couldn't remember the last time he'd been so at ease, and it made him dream. Maybe he could keep someone like Nic. Maybe they wouldn't have to hide a relationship much longer. It wasn't like they were in a corporate environment, and things were going so well with the kids, he couldn't imagine anything being extreme enough to affect his personal relationship with Nic. He was flying so high, not even his problems with his parents or his financial troubles could bring him down.

Today had been incredible, but spending all day tomorrow with Nic and the kids was bound to be the best day of his life.

Chapter Fifteen

Nic

THE alarm had gone off half an hour earlier, but Nic couldn't find it in him to rise yet. Yesterday had been a roller coaster, starting off with a welcome dose of Sasha. Everything about that man was sunny, even the way he smelled. He was the sweetest yet most virile male Nic had ever met, an enticing contradiction.

On one hand, he was the ultimate caretaker, bending over backward to make things right for everyone around him, generous and thoughtful. On the other, he was solid muscle and athletic, with a body built to perform and endure. Nothing was more beautiful than making that body submit, bend to Nic's will, and love every second of it. And Sasha did love it.

God, the way Sasha's body had shaken all over, held on a knife's edge of pleasure by Nic's will alone, had been more intoxicating than any high on the planet. Poor baby had fought so hard to stay silent, nearly clawing the seats. No matter how many times Nic had fought with himself, he couldn't cut himself off from Sasha. Every time he saw him, he wanted to get him naked and play with him all day long.

The other high of the day had been the kids. They'd never asked him to join in any family activities unless it was mandatory fun Nic had arranged, which was rare enough. It often seemed that Lucy and Ben were the family while Nic was some distant outlier, only there until the kids were old enough to move away, never to be seen again.

But they'd wanted him to join them last night. He'd had Sasha to thank for that. It had to be him inspiring them to pull together so much, to assemble all their broken pieces into a patchwork family. So it had been only fitting for Nic to reward him in the theater.

Unfortunately, it was now time to reward the kids by taking them to a mall to get some shopping done. Fuck, he hated crowded malls full of obnoxious people. The only positive aspects of this day would be having a driver so there'd be no parking frustrations and… and nothing. That was the only upside.

Nic prepared for retail battle, dressing in comfortable jeans and a pale green T-shirt with a crimson hoodie over it. For once, he threw on some tennis shoes. Who knew how many miles of mall he'd have to walk before Lucy and Ben were satisfied?

Swinging by his office, he ducked in to grab the wallet and cell phone he'd left on his desk. A flash of red caught his eye as he turned. Damned creepy elf.

He looked over his shoulder at the spindly thing at the edge of his desk. Only its ass and legs showed, the top half diving inside a large open bag of holiday M&M'S. That now-familiar warmth invaded him while he imagined Sasha sneaking into his office early and staging the candy diving scene. His man would wear a smile, thinking about Nic in this moment of discovery. *Fucking adorable.*

He hadn't imagined anyone would be ready before nine on a Sunday morning, but there they all were, sitting around the center island when he got to the kitchen. The sharp clatter of Sasha's coffee mug brought his gaze right to the man of his dreams. Sasha's bright blues were wide, his lips slightly parted, and his fingers frozen over where he'd dropped his cup.

Nic looked down his body and ran a hand down the front of him. "What? Do I have something on me?"

"Um." Sasha cleared his throat. "Well, no. Yes. Not really, but yes. You have clothes. I mean, like, real clothes, not a button-down or something."

Nic looked back up and grinned at Sasha. "Yeah, I've been known to wear clothes, Sasha."

Lucy giggled. "He's right, though, Uncle Nic. You never wear human clothes, only human-cloned android clothes."

He lifted his arms out to the sides. "Come on, Sasha. You've seen me in pajamas."

Sasha held up a palm. "I neither confirm nor deny. Okay, maybe one time." He gestured from head to foot along Nic's height. "This looks good on you. You should wear it more often."

As much attention as his own attire was getting, Nic was just as approving of Sasha's dark navy blue henley. The color made his eyes brighter and his hair blonder. A trim black leather jacket hung off the edge of the counter next to Sasha. Before he could make a fool of himself and demand Sasha put it on, he turned his eyes to the kids.

"Lucy, you're going to freeze in that," he said, nodding toward her. Her red dress wasn't *not* conservative, but it also had a too-short hem, in his opinion. "You expecting to impress someone when we get there?"

"Why, yes, Uncle Nic, and his name is Santa. If we go another year without a picture, I'll run away and join the circus. I'm almost too old to sit on Santa's lap."

"What do you mean almost?" Sasha asked.

Lucy threw a napkin at his head, which he caught without looking up. As if they did this often.

"It's clear weather out, so I thought we'd take the helicopter over and then hit University Village before it gets crappy out. That means get warm clothes, people."

Ben scoffed. "It's Washington. When isn't it crappy out?"

Nic hid his smile. "All right. The helo's been here for half an hour already. Get your stuff and let's go. Don't forget your credit cards. I don't want to deal with getting cash out for you kids, and I refuse to follow you around and wait in line to use my cards."

"Hey, Sasha, you been to U Village yet?" Ben asked, watching Sasha shake his head. "You're gonna like it there. There's a Stonehenge fountain, and the holiday lights are up, so when it gets dark, it'll be bright like the WildLights at the zoo."

"Nice! I can't wait to see it."

Nic's stomach flipped. He couldn't wait to show Sasha either. His enthusiasm for going out today leaped about a hundredfold all at once at the thought of showing Sasha something new. Plus, the kids seemed more alive than ever, talking and laughing and shoving each other a little as they headed out to the helipad area beside the house.

"Tesla's there, too, and Uncle Nic's going to let me test drive one today."

He looked over Ben's head at Sasha, shook his head, and mouthed *no*. Soon, they were all in the helicopter and then landed on the Leighton Price building, where they rode down the elevator and caught the town car to the shopping center.

It was a bit crowded, even this early on a Sunday, but the parking was always the worst thing about this center, and Nic never had to deal with that pain in the ass. They started out with coffee and pastries since some of the stores weren't open yet, but it didn't take long before Lucy and Ben were ready to run ahead and go their own ways. Nic let them off their leash with the requirement to keep their phones on, watch their belongings, stick together even when it was boring, and meet at an appointed time and place, the Stonehenge fountain in their case.

Once abandoned, Nic walked with Sasha, and occasionally one of them would stop to browse, though not often. Nic only wanted to soak in the company, walking close to Sasha, their hands brushing together. Finally, he took Sasha's hand in his and heard a contented sigh that made him smile. Sasha would never have taken his hand on his own—strong, smart, confident but often indecisive. It might have been their employer-employee relationship slowing Sasha down, not wanting to push too far, but part of Nic wanted to go too far with the golden boy.

They met up to have dinner at Din Tai Fung, where Sasha and Ben both swore they'd died and gone to dumpling heaven. Ben also spent a good twenty minutes complaining about having to stop at Sephora and Victoria's Secret, the latter being where he insisted shoppers were looking at him as if he were a pervert. Lucy said it was because he was fondling the bra cups, and Ben explained that they were exceedingly soft.

If Nic had thought yesterday had been a good day, this one was topping the list for best ever. The kids left again, but this time Nic told them to pay attention to their phones because he'd text them when and where to meet. Then he led Sasha to Fran's Chocolates where they selected some incredible artisan chocolates to take home, including jars of dark chocolate sauce and caramel sauce.

"I have ideas for these tonight," he whispered in Sasha's ear.

"Mm. You can't talk like that in my ear when I'm standing up," Sasha said. They found a seat on a bench near the big fountain, their thighs touching from hip to knee. "This feels good."

"It does." Nic tapped his foot against Sasha's. "I'm glad you came. This would suck without you here."

Sasha laughed. "You'd just sit in Starbucks on a laptop the whole time."

"Wow. How'd you know?"

"You were gone in your office a long time yesterday. I thought the contracts were all done."

"They are." Nic slid lower in the seat and tipped his head back, enjoying the cool evening air. Then he turned his head to look at Sasha. "Anselmo asked me to leave Leighton Price to partner with an Italian-owned, multinational business that wants to branch into the US."

Sasha's eyes widened. "That's incredible. Are you doing it?"

"No." He sighed.

"You look disappointed. If you want to do it, what's holding you back?"

"I don't have time. I've devoted my life to my career, and Leighton Price takes everything, too much of everything. I can't do both." Nic shook his head. "Fuck. This deal is exciting, promising. And I genuinely liked the De Francos. You remember them?"

"Uh, yeah, actually. The Christmas cookies, right?" Sasha grinned. "I can't get over those amaretti cookies Rossana made."

"Damn. I should have tried one. Anyway, I'd be working with Rossana's extended family, so Anselmo's in-laws, Matteo Basile and Turi Navarro. I did my homework on these guys, and they have an outstanding reputation. Their numbers are looking so hot right now too."

Sasha frowned. "Huh. So numbers get you off. Good to know." Nic nudged him, making him smile. Then his humor subsided. "Would it be such a bad thing to start something new? You don't seem particularly fulfilled where you are now."

Jaw clenching, Nic turned away and tried his best not to get defensive. "It's a family business."

"With only one family member working there."

"It's Ben's legacy."

"Really, Nic?" Sasha sat up straight. "Seriously? First of all, what about Lucy? A woman can't inherit the throne at Leighton Price, I take it? Second, have you met Ben? He's the most right-brained kid you'll ever meet. He'll be an artist, designer, or musician. He likes to wear tights and dance on a stage in front of crowds. Good luck getting him into a suit every day of his life."

"Fuck." Nic sat up, too, and dropped his head in his hands. Then, he felt Sasha's large hand on his shoulder, kneading into the muscle.

"You don't have to figure things out right this second," Sasha said. "There's time. Besides, look at the lights. Aren't they brilliant?"

That hand gave Nic's shoulder a light tug, drawing him back against the bench where Sasha's arm wrapped around him. With Sasha touching him, everything tended to feel right with the world.

"Hey, speaking of stages, the kids had some important things to say to you. After the retail coma they'll be in when we collect them, I doubt they'll think of it."

"Okay. What are they?"

"Well, first, Lucy has a holiday dance next week she'd like to go to. A boy she likes asked her. She seems to think you'd say no."

"She'd be right. No boys."

"Hmm. I wasn't expecting that. But she's sixteen, responsible, and has pretty damn good judgment. Are you sure you're not thinking of her as a little girl still?"

Nic hesitated. Had he been? How long did one beat the boys away? If only Josephine had shared any insights or even her own input on how she wanted her kids raised. He didn't want to make any more mistakes with them.

"Okay. We'll try it. With a curfew, of course."

"Of course. And Ben's doing his last musical on Tuesday night. Last chance to see him shine onstage. He's dying for you to come and watch his show before you never have another chance."

"Aw, fuck me," Nic said. "How do you do this? I hate musicals."

"Yeeeaah, they kind of make one feel uncomfortable sometimes, don't they? But you're not going to watch a musical. You're going to watch Ben."

He clapped his hand over his face. "All right. Sold. You should be a salesman."

"I kind of am. I sell learning opportunities to children who despise the education system. Gotta be a salesman or a magician to swing that."

Nic gazed at Sasha a long while as he people watched, making a few comments here and there. He was beautiful, unbelievably beautiful, right down to his center, and there was no way in hell Nic wasn't going to make love to him tonight.

"Hey, I think Santa's about to close up," Sasha said, frowning slightly as he caught Nic watching him. "Um, maybe we should call the kids."

"Oh yes. It's getting late." He checked his phone, but it was dead. "Damn. They might have been calling a while. I have no idea when my phone died."

"I got it." He texted Lucy, and within a few minutes, they met her and Ben and headed toward Santa's shop. Lucy was nearly running and had to keep coming back to rush everyone else along. Nic couldn't remember the last time she'd been so animated.

"C'mon, Uncle Nic. You are not getting out of this. Get in here." Lucy, the bully, waved him over like he was a mile away instead of a few feet. "There's a reason these are called family photos."

She ended up having to drag him in, but not because he was refusing. He simply couldn't move his feet at first, overwhelmed that they would want him there with them. Then he glanced at Sasha, whose wide grin lit him up inside even further as he nodded to Nic, urging him to join in. But he couldn't imagine this without Sasha—the entire reason this day existed.

He held out his hand. "Sasha."

"Nic." A tremor shook Sasha's voice. When the kids added their demands for him to jump into the shot, he jogged over. The second Sasha stood next to him, tucked against his side, Nic forgot the shoppers around them. Nothing existed but this time of laughing and photobombing and funny faces.

He never thought in a million years he'd end up getting pictures taken with Santa. There weren't many people left in line, so they had several poses, and Nic paid for all of them to be printed. Lucy did sit in Santa's lap, and Nic had to lay a restraining arm on Sasha, who insisted the guy had copped a feel of Lucy's butt.

When they heard about his decision to go to Ben's musical and to let Lucy go to her holiday dance, they went euphoric, throwing hugs around like they were free or something. Lucy said there was nothing left to ask Santa for, which made everyone laugh because she was always asking for more clothes or makeup or books. In fact, her room had more books than some people's libraries.

After cramming the bags that barely fit into the trunk of the town car, they made it back to the Leighton Price building at last and then flew back home. It had been a long, long day, and part of Nic was exhausted, mentally and physically. Another part of him rode the climbing anticipation of something momentous ahead of him.

The kids had begun to crash as soon as they'd gotten into the town car, so they said their good nights and went to their rooms almost immediately once they arrived. Nic wanted to go to bed, too, but not alone this time. No more unplanned, spontaneous interludes with Sasha. He was ready to bring him to his bed, to feel Sasha's skin from head to toe, to hold him in his arms and make love to him.

Leaving the shopping bags in the den, Nic took Sasha's hand and led him back along the first floor to his master suite, the largest bedroom in the house. As soon as they cleared the doors, Nic shut and locked them and backed Sasha to the prominent king-size bed, then pushed him onto it. Sasha's dazzling blue eyes never stopped tracking Nic as he grabbed lube and condoms and tossed them onto the bed.

"Seems like you have plans for me." Sasha practically quaked, lifting his head as he watched Nic and gripping the bedding beneath him in his fists. His voice had gone deep and raspy, and it inflamed Nic as intensely as it had that night in the movie theater.

"So many plans." Nic ran his hands from Sasha's hips to his abs and then to his shoulders, only to trace them slowly back down Sasha's body. "Now take off those clothes."

Sasha started to sit up, but Nic pressed him back down.

"No. Stay right where I put you and get naked."

"Jesus." Sasha's breathless reply and the excitement flaring in his expression sent a rush of exhilaration through Nic. It took every ounce of his restraint not to rip the clothes off both of them and pounce on Sasha.

Instead, Nic methodically stripped out of his own clothing a piece at a time, gradually revealing himself. He tried not to smile as Sasha fumbled every bit of his own undressing in his eagerness to please, lifting his hips and shimmying to wiggle his jeans down his legs. Sasha was already visibly trembling, but Nic wasn't far off from doing the same. This was the first time they would be naked together, free to touch and explore. Bare,

Sasha was a work of art worthy of a museum exhibit. His muscles were defined, sleek, bunching and releasing with every movement, and Nic couldn't wait any longer.

Bending forward, Nic braced one arm on the bed and cupped Sasha's jaw with the other hand. One day's worth of stubble prickled his palm as he stroked down to Sasha's nape. Holding him in place, Nic lowered his lips to Sasha. Their kiss began tender, as it often did. It also never lasted before the fire between them consumed them, driving them deeper and harder, desperate for more.

Within minutes, Nic was already short of breath and abandoning all thought of planning a seduction. Impulse alone drove him.

"I need you on me," Sasha rasped. "Please, Nic. I need to feel you."

Nic directed Sasha farther onto the bed and lowered on top of him at last, pushing between Sasha's legs. At last, Nic had Sasha's hard body beneath him with his hot skin, breathy sighs of pleasure, and hands gliding down Nic's back, fingertips pressing into skin. Wrapping his arms around Sasha, Nic took his mouth again until he was dizzy with need. He broke away and kissed a path down Sasha's throat, along his collarbone, over his pecs. He freed one hand to trace his fingers through the golden hair on Sasha's chest until he stopped at Sasha's nipples. His mouth sucking and licking one, he attended to the other with his fingers, gently pinching and caressing.

Sasha ground his hips against Nic, his breath coming in pants. Pleasure exploded through Nic as their cocks glided together. He rose up to more fully align with Sasha's length and then gripped them both with one hand, stroking them together.

"Oh fuck." Sasha lifted his legs around Nic's hips, the thick muscles flexing and quivering. Suddenly, Nic

wanted those legs higher, over his shoulders, while he
sank inside of Sasha. Then Sasha's eyes opened, and
everything shrank in on him and Sasha until there was
nothing else in the world that mattered. Those ocean
eyes sucked Nic in and drowned him in possibilities
and long-lost hopes discovered.

Nic kissed him like the world was going to end
tomorrow. While he did, he patted the bed beside him
until he found the lube he'd thrown there earlier, and
then he sat up.

"Hey, where are you going?"

Nic laughed. "Nowhere. There's no way in hell I'd
want to walk away from this." He dragged his fingers
through the sprinkle of golden chest hair over Sasha's
pecs and traced the line down his happy trail.

A smile crossed Sasha's face, but there was a
vulnerability to it that tightened the center of Nic's chest.
It fired up a powerful desire to protect Sasha, to care for
him and make up for all the times no one else had. They
might not be ready for that yet in their relationship, but
Nic was damn sure going to take care of him physically.

He pushed at Sasha's inner thighs. "Wider. Now,
Sasha."

Instantly following the command, Sasha complied,
wonderfully responsive as always, like his only pleasure
was to give pleasure. Nic coated his fingertips and
enjoyed Sasha's hiss of delight as he explored and
probed Sasha before carefully sliding his finger into him.
He bent down and sucked the head of Sasha's cock into
his mouth, making Sasha's ab muscles jump.

After a few strokes, he backed off. "Look at you,"
Nic said. "You are perfectly groomed down here."

He played with Sasha's sac while gradually
stretching Sasha with his finger. As he slowly worked a

second one in, he lowered his mouth and sucked Sasha's delicate skin, working his tongue and lips all over Sasha's balls and then moving up to his cock again. He smelled good, tasted good, clean and musky and all man.

Sasha's grip tightened in Nic's hair, and ragged moans burst from above Nic's head. "I can't," he panted. "I'm ready. I can't wait anymore. Please, Nic."

But Nic loved drawing it out for Sasha. He loved the beauty of his anticipation, the tension, of the quivering mess of him waiting for release and his wild abandon when it was granted.

It was the desperate chant that broke him, though.

"Fuck me, fuck me, fuck me." Sasha's eyes were squeezed shut, his breath racing, and his hips thrusting onto Nic's fingers.

A dam burst in him, a volcanic clawing low in his groin, and it unleashed his restraint. He sat up to lube his condom-covered cock and then replaced his fingers with it. It took every ounce of willpower to keep from slamming right into Sasha.

Nic lifted Sasha's legs higher, opening him more, and rocked slowly into him. Sasha let out a long groan as Nic sank deeper with each movement.

"Sasha." He waited for Sasha's eyes to open. "Tell me you're okay."

Sasha's hands slid up Nic's forearms to hold on to his biceps. "I'm—ah, that's so good—I'm fucking amazing. Don't stop, Nic."

The house would have to collapse before he stopped now. He was beyond stopping. Finally, he was fully inside Sasha's hot, tight channel. Nic leaned forward, covering Sasha, bracing with one arm and tucking his other arm beneath Sasha's trembling thigh, pressing him deep into the mattress.

"Ready, Sasha? Want my dick?"

"So ready," he whispered against Nic's throat. "I want all of it."

It was all Nic needed. He withdrew to his tip and thrust back in hard, making Sasha grunt. Again he thrust and again, faster and faster, his heart racing and his breath heaving. His balls began to tighten up, and the burning pleasure began at the base of his spine. He wasn't going to last long. He shoved his left hand farther under Sasha's ass to lift him more, changing the angle.

"Yessss," Sasha hissed, and then he cried out, his movements going jerky. "Oh fuck, I love that. Right there, Nic. Harder."

Nic spread his own legs wider and then pushed harder until he was practically pounding against Sasha's asscheeks in a rapid rhythm, the slap of skin on skin driving him wild. Sweat slicked his body, heat flushing every inch. Never had he felt so alive, everything sizzling with sensation.

"Fuck!" His fingers were slipping on Sasha's damp skin. He took a firmer grip and dropped his head to nip Sasha's inner thigh near his knee. "Come now, Sasha. I need you to come all over me."

Nic slid his hand from Sasha's ass to his hard cock, squeezing and stroking his velvety flesh. Another nip and lick and Sasha went off with a long, deep cry, and thick come painted his belly.

"Goddamn, Sasha," he gasped. Sasha's ass tightened around Nic, shoving him headfirst over the edge of bliss. He dropped onto Sasha, clutching that sweet body to him as his own body seized, overtaken with penetrating pulses of ecstasy. A moment later, he withdrew from inside Sasha and rolled them to the side, their arms still around each other.

A tired laugh escaped Sasha. "Is it cheesy if I say that was transcendental?"

Nic's arms tightened around him. "Yeah, it is, but it was."

As he came down from the high of his orgasm, he leaned his head against the side of Sasha's. This was the hardest part, the sex being the easiest. Should they sleep in their separate rooms? Did he want Sasha to spend the night with him? Was this a one-time thing, or should they continue their affair?

No simple answers came to him. To his surprise, he did want Sasha to stay here in his arms, very much so. He shouldn't, though, and the fact remained, he couldn't invite him to.

He kissed Sasha's temple. "I'll be right back."

Nic went to the attached master bathroom to rid himself of the condom and take care of business, all the while trying to find a painless way to send Sasha to his own room. When he came out, Sasha was already half-dressed, sitting on the bed to pull his shoes on.

Smiling at Nic, he nodded toward Nic's groin. "I didn't expect that."

He laughed. Yes, he had a semi already. "It's standard when you're around."

Joking aside, there was longing in Sasha's eyes. Sasha wanted to stay overnight. He just knew better than to ask, and as usual, he made this easier for everyone because that's what he always had to do.

Nic's heart lurched in his chest. He strode over to kneel on the bed, straddling Sasha's lap, cradling his head, and kissed the fuck out of him. Sasha opened up like a blossom under Nic's mouth. They were both breathless at the end, leaning their foreheads together.

"Don't start something we can't finish," Sasha murmured. Nic chuffed out a laugh.

"Yeah." He backed off Sasha's lap so he could finish dressing and then climbed onto the middle of the bed, drawing the bedspread partly over him. "It's sad to cover all that up."

"Meh. I could be bulkier. Maybe Percy has a good tip or two."

Nic smacked Sasha's back lightly with a pillow. "Don't you dare talk to Percy about his tip."

It worked to lighten the mood a little. Sasha finished dressing and leaned in to kiss Nic one more time. "Parting is such sweet sorrow," he said with a sassy grin.

Nic snorted and gave him a little shove. "Teachers."

Sasha was laughing as he went out the door to head to his own room, but his words weren't far off. Really, Nic couldn't put a finger on why any shred of melancholy had darkened their night. It had been earth-shattering sex after a fantastic day. They should both be happy, and Nic was. How could this not be enough for him? And why the fuck did this feel so much like an ending?

Chapter Sixteen

Sasha

HE should never have left Nic Sunday night. It had been the biggest mistake of Sasha's life, or maybe indulging his enormous emotional attachment to Nic had been the true mistake. He wasn't ready to label himself as used, but he was nearly there. Two days of no contact should have made that clear to Sasha, but none of this made sense.

Nic hadn't seemed like the kind of guy to play with a man's head, to fuck him and leave him, especially when they were supposed to have a working relationship that couldn't be ignored. Yet Sasha had been ignored. For two days.

And then tonight had been the sure indication of trouble. They'd just arrived home from Ben's musical, which Nic had been painfully absent from. Ben was devastated, enough that he let Sasha tuck him against his side. He curved his arm around the boy, who'd been fighting away so-called unmanly tears all evening.

"I'm sure there wasn't a choice, Ben. He wouldn't do that to you on purpose or if he could avoid it. You know that, right?"

Ben shrugged under his arm. Lucy was too furious to speak, and after gushing about how wonderful Ben's performance as Joseph had been, she stormed to her room, leaving them alone.

"Percy usually goes, and he wasn't even there." Ben's voice wobbled.

"Well, I think that's a good indication something serious kept Nic from coming tonight."

Ben shoved up from the sofa. "It doesn't matter," he mumbled.

After he'd gone, Sasha braced his elbows on his knees and dropped his head into his hands. A sick feeling twisted inside his stomach without any sign of leaving. Neither Nic nor Percy had returned any of Sasha's messages. He fought the negativity that threatened to overcome him, to drag him into a pit of despair, but it was eating him alive.

Maybe there was nothing going wrong between him and Nic. Maybe it was only bad timing that Nic dropped out of communication right after they'd had sex. But that wasn't Sasha's kind of luck. One of the worst things was his absolute lack of power to do anything about the situation. The imbalance between him and Nic had never been clearer.

Should he even bother waiting up to see if Nic was coming home tonight? He'd tried that last night already, and it had only resulted in fatigue and escalating anxiety. Repeatedly, his evening with Nic played in his mind, but nothing about it warranted this complete shutdown between them. Had second thoughts driven Nic away?

Stupid. His dumb ass shouldn't have talked about his financial problems or his issues with his parents. Nic might have thought Sasha was angling for money or something. It was possible Nic had run into gold diggers plenty of times before. He could imagine the discussion about finances coming off as uncomfortable, though at the time, Nic hadn't seemed to think anything bad of it. Even if it wasn't about the money, maybe dumping his problems on Nic had been a mistake.

Whatever the issue, sitting on the sofa all night wasn't going to solve it. He had no choice but to wait for Nic to make an appearance and explain why he'd ghosted Sasha. As he headed up to his suite, guilt gnawed at him on top of his own confusion and fears. Would Nic have skipped out on the musical to avoid Sasha? If so, it was on Sasha's head that Ben was so hurt and betrayed. So much for being a positive influence on the kids.

Sasha curled up on his bed fully clothed when he got to his suite, too emotionally drained to do much more. He spent the night tossing and turning, occasionally drifting off only to jerk awake at every little noise in the house, every notification popping up on his phone. He was up early to make breakfast for Ben and Lucy, but neither came to the kitchen until it was nearly time for them to leave for school. They were both subdued and only grabbed granola bars and fruit before racing to meet the driver out front. They had his empathy.

Trying to force food past his own nonexistent appetite, he managed a few bites of cereal and a small glass of juice, but it was his chest that felt hollow and needing fulfillment, not his stomach. It was simple to think he wouldn't be suffering through this if he hadn't gotten involved with Nic, but then, he also wouldn't have had the best couple of weeks of his life either. Part of him still held hope he could work out whatever mystery problem had worked its way between them over the last three days.

He did the only thing that could possibly ease him. He ran. Then he kept going beyond his usual distance as if demons were at his heels. When he returned, more exhausted than ever, he showered and dressed and then cleaned the kitchen right before messing it all up again to make something special for Lucy's big night. He'd decided on a caramel apple cheesecake because she was a complete freak for anything with cheesecake in it. After he'd gotten it in the oven, set the timer, and cleaned the kitchen once more, he made some phone calls.

The first was to have the dress and accessories Lucy had selected sent over. The next was to confirm Lucy's appointment with her favorite stylist to do her hair and makeup. Then he checked her dinner reservations at the Hardware Store Restaurant, Lucy's favorite, and as a surprise, arranged for a special limo to drive her and Damian in case the boy didn't have anything set up.

By the time he was done, his timer had gone off, so he pulled the cheesecake out to cool. He glanced at his watch; there were too many hours left in the day. Without any purpose or place to be, he crept up to his room and tried to nap without any luck.

A half hour later when his phone rang, he nearly pounced on it, but it was McMurray, Ben's school. He frowned and answered. Then he cussed a streak after hanging up. Ben had skipped school. Again. Nic was going to be furious, no question about it. He had never hidden how extremely important he considered the kids' schooling.

Sasha had to find him quickly. After throwing on a thick, zippered Seahawks hoodie and a pair of tennis shoes, he raced down to the front door and out to the garage where he threw caution to the wind and hopped in his truck instead of waiting for a driver. The first place he thought to go was Crow Beach. Ben had shown great interest in photography once he'd gotten a good look at Sasha's camera, and they'd talked about it quite a lot. It was then that Ben had mentioned the crows and the sunset views of Mount Rainier in the distance. Clearly, it was a haven of peace for Ben. Apparently, he'd needed that haven today too.

Sasha found Ben sitting on a large log of driftwood. The kid's shoulders slumped as he watched the water.

"Whatever you're looking for, you won't find it out there," Sasha said as he dropped onto the driftwood next to Ben.

"I never should have told you about this place."

"You'd rather cops come to find you?"

With a snort, Ben shook his head. "I can't sit in class right now."

"Why not?" Sasha asked. "And don't give me that generic crap about hating it and the classes being useless. What are you feeling when you sit there that makes you want to run away from it?"

Ben finally turned his head and looked at Sasha. The kid's eyes were red-rimmed, which cut Sasha's guts like he'd swallowed broken glass. "I don't know. Restless? I can't sit there. I'm so full of... something. Like I'm going to burst."

"And you want to yell and cry and hit things? Something like that?"

He nodded in response, and Sasha put an arm over his shoulder.

"That's okay, and it's normal. No one ever wants to hear these words, but it'll pass, and it will get better."

"That's bullshit," he said. Sasha ignored the language and focused on Ben's expression as he said it. Cynical, hopeless, but mostly sad.

"You've felt like this a long time, haven't you?"

Ben lifted his head and sent Sasha a look of surprise before nodding. "Things were finally going okay since you got here."

"And then last night happened," Sasha finished.

"He still hasn't said anything. I don't think he cares about us."

Sasha could relate, but the kids were family. They'd been with Nic for years, and he was a parent now whether he wanted to deny the role or not. Maybe Sasha had fucked up with Nic somewhere along the line, but the kids deserved better treatment than this.

"I don't believe that, Ben. I really don't." He squeezed Ben's shoulder. "I'm thinking he's struggling with a lot right now. He has so many responsibilities, more than he ever lets on, and he's trying to keep a balance without having anything drop. Like juggling, you know. It's impossible to expect nothing to drop. He tries, but he's human. Sometimes he fails."

"But he drops us a lot."

"Does he? Are you ever without food, shelter, clothes?" He waited for Ben to shake his head. "Don't you have a clean house, good food, and reliable people to help care for you?" An answering nod. "Does he neglect your education because your future doesn't matter?" Another shake of his head. "When you ask for something, does he deny you? And before you bring up the musical, think about how many times you've actually asked him to be there."

A long pause and then Ben shook his head. "I didn't think about that. We tell him about events. I can't remember ever inviting him to any."

A relieved sigh swept Sasha. That was exactly what he needed Ben to see. "No, he's never invited. Imagine him losing his sister and then finding out he needed to be a parent. He wasn't prepared. Would he feel good enough to step into those shoes, especially with you two grieving and in pain? Do you think he's ever felt good enough?"

"But he doesn't have to be them," Ben said.

"What is it you want from him, Ben?"

Tears pooled in the boy's eyes. "I just want him to be around. I want…."

"You want him to love you," Sasha said. Ben nodded, ducking his head against Sasha's shoulder to hide his tears, his curly hair tickling Sasha's throat and chin. "Sometimes to get love, you have to give it. I know you had a good time with Nic this past weekend and with the game night. You can have more of that. Ben, you can tell him you love him. You can invite him in. He needs it as much as you do. He's been hovering outside of you and Lucy for a long time, and it's gotta be cold out there."

Ben sniffled. "Are you sure?"

"About this? Heck yeah, I'm sure. Watch and see. Ask him to eat with you. Ask him to spend time with you, to take you places you want to go. Ask him for advice.

For Christ's sake, Ben, hug him. He's not wrapped in an untouchable bubble, and he's not mean like your grandparents. I promise you, he won't turn you away."

With a sob, Ben threw his arms around Sasha's ribs tightly, and then he whispered, "Thanks, Sasha. I'm ready to go home now."

"Not school?"

He laughed. "It's a short day because of an assembly. Unless you want me to go back for that?"

"Nah. Let's go home."

As it turned out, they'd been talking a while, and school would have been nearly out anyway. Ben spent the short ride home completely psyched about riding in Sasha's lifted beast of a truck, making him glad he'd decided to drive himself. He'd collected many of his best memories in this cab. Now he could add Ben to the collection.

Ben headed to his room as soon as he got in, but Sasha froze as he was about to pass the den when he saw Percy lounging in there with his feet propped on the coffee table. He rose from the sofa when he saw Sasha.

Sasha's heart thumped a staccato rhythm before leveling out again. He met Percy halfway across the room.

"I've been leaving messages." He didn't quite know what to do with his hands, so he shoved them into the front pockets of his jeans. The way Percy looked at him but didn't meet his eyes had him on edge.

Percy sighed. "I know. I'm sorry."

The pause stretched his nerves to a breaking point. "What the fuck's going on, Percy? Please, just spit it out."

With his arms crossed, Percy's shoulders dropped. "There's no easy way to say this, Sasha, but you're fired. How long will it take you to pack up? I can have house staff help you if you need it."

The sick feeling in him blew up to outright nausea. He swallowed a few times, his face flushing with heat as he fought a battle with his stomach. "Why? What happened?"

"Look, Monday he wanted you gone. He didn't explain why, but there was a lot going on that day, a business emergency. Someone slapped his newest acquisition in Italy with a patent lawsuit. The news hit, and everyone panicked. He wasn't available Sunday, so a bunch of clients took their business elsewhere by Monday. We lost millions in sales overnight."

"It was only one day."

"Bad shit happens fast, and the pressure for instant response is high at his level in the company. It wasn't only the distraction, Sasha. He got a message that Ben ditched school today."

"I talked to Ben. I don't think it'll be a—"

"Do you know why I'm home right now when Nic needs me at work fighting for the company with him?"

He shook his head, his throat too tight and achy to respond.

"Lucy got in a fight at school. You weren't answering your phone, so I had to pick her up. She's been suspended. I shouldn't have to add she's not going to the dance tonight." Percy dropped his hands to his hips. "I'm really sorry, Sasha. I don't think this is your fault. It's horrible timing, and Nic's more wrecked than I've ever seen him. He couldn't take on more problems, and he got slammed with two strikes today."

"And he couldn't tell me himself?" His fists clenched as pain blew his heart to pieces. "Not even a call?"

"Like I said, he doesn't need more problems. He always has me deal with employee issues. Don't take it personally."

"He wasn't just—" He choked on the words, and his vision blurred. "Oh God, Percy, we weren't just—"

He doesn't need more problems. That's all Sasha ever was to everyone, wasn't he? Too much of a burden. Too much trouble. How did he keep letting this happen? He couldn't even blame Nic for this. Sasha had been the failure who couldn't keep the kids happy. Devastating misery brought Sasha to his knees, his head cradled in his hands.

"*Fuck.* Goddamn you, Nic," he heard Percy whisper above him. Then, Percy's arms came around him, his big body covering Sasha's back, and he couldn't hold back the agony anymore. He let himself cry, let out the silent sobs racking his body while Percy held him. Who the fuck cared now? There was only Percy, and a rejection from him, too, couldn't possibly top Nic's.

He had no home, no job, no family, no money. He had nowhere to turn and a macerated heart painting the crater in his chest where a whole one used to be. Of everything, that was the worst. He'd let himself feel too much for Nic. His entire life having to take care of himself, he'd never been a quitter. So, he'd pick himself up and survive, find a home and a job.

But Nic could never be replaced. The bloody mass in his chest would just have to stay obliterated for a while.

Chapter Seventeen

Nic

SLOUCHING in his office chair, Nic stared out the window over the Seattle nightscape with his glass dangling from his fingers. His suit was a mess, shoes off, the tie long gone, and shirt unbuttoned to his collarbone. It was so late, no one would be around to see. Such had been his week, working until he passed out with his head on his desk. Few of his executives worked Saturdays, much less into the evening, even with the company scrambling.

Nothing had been right since his night with Sasha last Sunday. After Sasha left, he'd plugged in his dead phone, and then the deluge had begun. Missed call after missed call, text upon text. It took all night to piece together all the events and effects of everything. Then, he'd had to fly to the Leighton Price building, consult his legal department, gather his resources, calculate the effects, and come up with a battle plan.

The patent lawsuit against the Italian leather supplier had begun on Friday. Why he hadn't heard anything about it until late on Sunday was still undetermined, but he assumed the managers had tried to deal with the problem before alerting Leighton Price. That had been the first mistake because the news had several days to ruminate, and when no one responded to his clients' concerns, they began maneuvering out of contracts. The domino effect began, more and more businesses pulling out, worried that Leighton Price couldn't meet production guarantees.

Nic had watched all his hard work slip away like it had merely been a dream. If only he'd been home working like he usually was. If only he hadn't been distracted by something as frivolous as a shopping trip and fucking ridiculous pictures with Santa. His phone wouldn't have died if he hadn't been out all day. He might have saved some of the contracts, probably most of them, if he'd gotten his messages.

He downed the rest of his scotch and gathered his belongings before flying home for the first time all week. Yes, he'd had a lot of work, but not enough to warrant staying away so long. At least Sasha wouldn't be there. It would have been nearly impossible to face him. Percy had mentioned he'd left the same night he'd been…. Fuck, he could barely even think the words.

He'd *fired* Sasha and practically kicked him out of the house. And sort of broke up with him. They hadn't officially been together, but how much more official could it be than family outings and evenings in, heavy make-out sessions, and long, hard, mind-blowing sex? He'd ended everything professional and personal with Sasha without taking the time to do it face-to-face.

At the time, he'd been so out of his head with fear and anger, imagining the end of everything he'd built all his life, and he'd struck out at anyone within reach, including Sasha. Now that rash decision plagued him, clawing deeper and deeper into his conscience.

Every day, he'd have to look at that sofa, the kitchen, his own bed, and try not to picture Sasha there, know he'd never see him there again. He gasped as a punch of pain caught him unexpectedly.

But as much as he wanted Sasha, wanted to make up for his fucked-up treatment of Sasha, it was better to leave things as they were. Percy had found a temporary replacement nanny, a more proper one, which was particularly important now that school was out for Christmas break. Judging from the incidents the past week with the kids, having Sasha around hadn't helped change their behavior.

Sasha had disrupted not only the household but also Nic's focus on work. Now, his parents hadn't returned to the house, his position was in even more jeopardy, and the business was in danger of running in the red for the first time since its inception. Everything had been going so smoothly. Until it wasn't. Then it had seemed clear the situation with Sasha wasn't working out.

Nic found Percy waiting for him in the den when he got home. His friend had been around nearly constantly the last few days yet not truly present at all, which was an odd thing to think but apt. No doubt Percy had a lot of opinions rolling around waiting to burst free. It wasn't the first time, but he usually let Nic have it sooner than later.

When Nic grabbed a drink and sat across from him, Percy didn't speak for a long while, another thing out of character for him. Yet Nic waited. After all, he'd been trained to deal with difficult business associates during negotiations. Since when had Percy become someone he needed to dance around?

Even knowing the tactic, he couldn't stand any more. "Your disapproval is noted." Nic stood up. "Have a good night, Percy."

"Oh, sit the fuck down, dickhead." Percy paused until Nic sat. "Why'd you have to put your damn hands on him, Nic? You've never fucked around with employees before."

The question had been ringing in his own thoughts over the past week. As always, no answer came to mind. Sasha had been a magnetic force with an attraction he hadn't been able to deny.

He dropped his head back on the sofa and blindly stared at the ceiling. "I don't know why. Because I couldn't *not* put them on him. Percy, I didn't want to want him, to like him. Complicating my life wasn't the plan."

"Funny thing, though. I like him, too, so I don't appreciate the position you put me in. Imagine my surprise when I found out he was more than just your kids' caretaker. Firing employees is something I can deal with, but this was personal. So you could, what? Uncomplicate your life? Fine. I eviscerated him for you, Nic. And then I was the one who held him right there on the floor where he was gutted."

Percy pointed at a place near the end of the sofas, and Nic could almost see Sasha there, confused, hurt, rejected. He wanted to look away, but he deserved to feel the consequences. God, there was so much he wanted to take back.

He turned his eyes back to Percy. "I'm sorry I didn't tell you. I'm sorry I sent you to do it. It's too late to undo anything."

Dropping his feet from the low coffee table to the floor, Percy leaned forward. "It's not too late to talk to Sasha and get him back."

For one moment, the idea of that blazed through his mind, but reality was a bitch. "You can't be serious. The way I did it was horrible, wrong, but it wasn't wrong to separate from him. Everything became so messed up because of my relationship with him."

"You really think that?" Percy's brows rose.

He nodded. "Yeah, I do."

"Your logic is seriously flawed here," Percy said. "Are you sure you're not running scared?"

"Fuck no, I'm not running."

"Right. He didn't push your boundaries at all, make you want things you weren't raised to want." The sarcasm nearly dripped from Percy's words. "Well, you might as well send everyone who makes you uncomfortable out of your life."

"What do you mean?"

"The boarding school for the kids. I sent the information to your email, and there's a file in your office. Only one stood out without sending the kids out of the state, and it's the Annie Wright School in Tacoma. They board all ages and genders. You should love it. It gets them far enough away you'll almost never have to see them."

A sharp cry got both of their attention. Lucy stood frozen right inside the den entry, her expression horrified. "You're getting rid of us too?" She didn't wait for an answer but turned and bolted from the room.

"Christ." Nic drew his hands over his face. "She thinks I'm sending her and Ben away."

"Weren't you?"

He glared at Percy. "I get that you're mad at me right now, but I wasn't sure about the boarding school yet. I was frustrated because I've tried everything to get through to them. Nothing was working, but then—"

Jolting forward, he gripped the sofa on either side of his legs. A sharp exhale burst out of him as an epiphany ripped him apart. He shook his head over and over, his breath growing shorter.

"No. Fuck no. *He* got through." Nic looked up. "What am I doing to myself? I don't want to be my parents, Percy."

He'd spent most of his childhood in boarding schools, isolated, abandoned, excluded. He'd never been good enough to satisfy his parents, never disciplined enough, focused enough. Putting Lucy and Ben into the same mold would ruin them like it had him, and for Josephine's sake, he couldn't allow that to happen to her children.

Percy stood and waved toward the hallway. "Then go talk to them about it. Reassure them. And for God's sake, why don't you think about fixing things with Sasha?"

The thought of facing Sasha after hurting him made Nic's heart pound. Everything in him ached to have Sasha back, but he couldn't stop thinking about how his life had fallen apart so quickly after meeting him.

When he got upstairs, Lucy wasn't in her room, but he heard her voice farther down the hall. Ben's bedroom door was ajar, and he was crying openly with big, messy sobs. Lucy had an arm around his shoulders, trying to comfort him.

Nic stepped inside and closed the door. "I'm sorry you heard that downstairs, Lucy. Percy was a little harsh because he's angry with me. You two aren't going anywhere. Ever. I'm not sending anyone away."

She glared up at him, tears shimmering in her eyes too. "You think that's what this is about? I didn't tell Ben about any of what I heard."

He shook his head, his eyes narrowing. "You didn't? Then, what—"

"What'd you do to Sasha?" Ben shouted. His face was blotchy and his eyes puffy when he looked up.

"Ben, I didn't *do* anything to Sasha," he said. Both kids condemned him with their eyes, full of anger and something close to grief. "He wasn't working out. You two were still getting in trouble at school."

"What? I don't believe you," Lucy cried. She jumped up from where she sat on Ben's bed, strode forward, and pointed her finger close to Nic's face. "You think Sasha had anything to do with Ben skipping school? He did it before Sasha got here. He stopped when Sasha got here. Magically, he did it again when *you* ditched his musical. Did you know neither of us is failing classes anymore because of Sasha? Did you know how often he had to defend you to us every day like your own personal white knight?"

By the time she stopped, her shoulders were shaking and her face was wet. She shoved against Nic's chest with her slender hands. Then she shoved again and again.

"He was different. He loved us." One final shove actually moved Nic back an inch. "*He loved you!* How could you toss him away like he wasn't anything special?"

Grabbing a tissue from Ben's desk nearby, she dropped into the desk chair and wiped her face. Her words shredded what was left of his heart.

"You knew?" he whispered.

"Knew what?" Ben asked, but Lucy nodded.

"Uncle Nic, I'm almost an adult, and I'm a woman. Of course I knew. All it took was seeing the way you two looked at each other."

"No way!" His eyes widening with understanding, Ben moved to lean against his desk next to Lucy. "You and Sasha? Then, why would you fi—"

"It's complicated, Ben." Nic turned to Lucy. "I don't know that having him here was good for me."

"Yes, it was," she said without hesitation. "For the first time, I felt like this was a home, but mostly, I felt like you were part of it. That was one of Sasha's magical powers."

Nic sank down onto one of Ben's bean bag chairs and rubbed a hand over his face. Lucy had never looked so disappointed in him, and Ben had gotten a hopeful look on his face. She put a hand on Ben's arm, though.

"Don't get your hopes up, Ben. Sasha didn't fit into Uncle Nic's sense of order around the house." Her words held barbs much like Percy's had. "He wasn't perfect enough. He was too messy. He was too loud. He was too…."

She continued, but he couldn't follow them further. Watching Ben's face fall was hard enough, but it was those barbs that hooked Nic's guts and spilled them. Those were his parents' words, what they would say about Sasha, what they'd said about Nic when he was a child, too boisterous and active to please them. *I don't want to be my parents.* Well, he was certainly doing a great job following in their footsteps.

"That's not true," he said, cutting her off. "What you said, it wasn't true. He *is* perfect."

She leaned forward and grabbed his forearms. "Then why are you waiting? He could be long gone from here, getting farther away from us."

"Please," Ben rasped. "Don't let him go, Uncle Nic."

Pushing himself out of the seat, he headed to the door and then looked back. "I can only try. I don't know if he'll come back."

When he walked out, he was followed by cheers, but they didn't soothe him as he entered his home office and sat at his desk. The way he'd treated Sasha had to have left a wound, and on top of everything, a voice deep inside warned him to protect himself, that everything he'd worked for was in jeopardy because of his feelings for Sasha.

Then his eyes fell on that silly fucking elf hanging halfway out of the bag of candy. Nearly a week and the little fellow hadn't moved from the edge of Nic's desk, a painful reminder of Sasha's absence. Before last weekend, Nic had seen that elf strapped down to a Lego board with little men all around it, in a miniature bed with naked Barbies, and frozen in a block of ice with a marshmallow snowman. In a million years, he never thought he'd miss seeing that creepy elf in a new position.

He could at least find out where Sasha went. Pulling out his phone, he saw several messages had come in, and the familiar panic set in, a reminder of late Sunday night when his world had crashed and burned. When he listened to the voicemails, he ran a gamut of emotions.

First, the head of his legal team said they'd reached an agreement with the plaintiff, who then dropped the lawsuit. Then Percy called to say he'd gotten the message about the suit and was able to recover most of the contracts. Then, a call came from Anselmo. He expressed sympathy for the troubles he'd heard about with Leighton Price. He then pledged to double his contracts with Nic. The final message was his father, a long, scathing message. Nic hung up before his father's rant was finished, something he'd never dreamed of doing before.

He started to put his head down on his desk, relief and frustration hitting at once, when he noticed the files in the middle of it. Nic opened one. The Annie Wright information was there. The school seemed amazing, but if he knew one thing, it was that sending the kids away would be one of his biggest fuckups ever. He tossed the file in the waste bin.

Flicking the other file open, his stomach flipped. Sasha's smile stood out from their pictures with Santa. They were all smiling, even him. Had he ever appeared happy in any of his photos before? He braced his head in his hands, a deep, piercing ache spreading through him like a poison. There was no lying to himself as he found Sasha in each picture. He loved that face. He loved that man.

Of all the crap Nic had laid at Sasha's feet, none of it had been Sasha's fault. He'd been amazing with the kids, amazing with Nic, and nothing that happened at Leighton Price had a damned thing to do with Sasha. Yet Nic had blamed him. A week later, the lawsuit was dropped and more than enough contracts recovered to restore the numbers to where they needed to be.

Those fucking numbers. It was all he lived for, enough to neglect the children he was supposed to nurture, enough to annihilate the man he'd fallen in love with, enough to condemn himself daily to a job he hated and turn away the opportunity for something more, something better. *Enough.* He'd had more than enough. His father could go fuck himself. Nic couldn't live that way anymore. It wasn't a life plan but an early grave guarantee.

He was in pain, the kids were in pain, and Sasha was—where? He had no idea. As if his guilt weren't burning enough in his skull, sharp awareness sank in of how badly he'd hurt Sasha. Nic had known about Sasha's trouble with his parents. Broke and homeless, where would Sasha go? No one ever took care of Sasha. Nic had promised himself from the start that he would be different, that he'd take care of him. But he hadn't. In the midst of his own shitstorm, he'd forgotten what Sasha needed.

Fuck. He jumped up, urgency thundering through his veins. It had been days. Was he on the street somewhere? In a shelter? Living in his truck? *Fuck, fuck, fuck.* He sped to Percy's door, thumping on it without an answer and then pushing it open. The water was running in the bathroom, so he swung the door open. Percy's reflection stared at him with disbelief, a towel wrapped around his hips and shaving cream over half of his face.

"The fuck?" he blurted.

Nic ignored him. "Wow, is that a new tattoo? Hard to tell when you're covered in them." He brought his eyes back to the reflection of Percy's face. "I need help finding Sasha. Right now."

"Well, it's about time." Percy relaxed, turned his gaze back to the mirror, and continued shaving.

"Hey, I'm fucking serious. I need to fucking find him right fucking now before I fucking go insane."

Percy laughed.

"If anything happens to him before—"

"Oh, so now you care?" He whipped around to face Nic. "You have a conscience now?"

Nic got right in Percy's face. "If you think I haven't been in hell since last weekend, you're blind. I don't eat. I don't sleep. I've raked myself over the coals every single fucking day. It was like chewing off my own limb to escape the chain and make him leave, Percy. You know damn well I couldn't even face him to do it. Only I was a stupid, *stupid* man. He wasn't chaining me. He was holding me." He spun and began pacing the length of the bathroom. "I'm a moron. I've been rich since the day I was born, dammit. It never crossed my mind he wouldn't be able to pay rent or buy food or—Christ, I have to find him. I want him back."

Grabbing his shoulder, Percy held him in place. "You mean it? You aren't going to toss him out in a month or two when you get scared again? Because I swear to all that's unholy, if you—"

"I fucking mean it. I want him. I need to take care of him." Nic sighed when Percy looked skeptical. "No matter what happens between us, I will take care of him. Please, Percy. I'm worried about him."

Something in Nic's face must have convinced Percy because he rinsed the shaving cream away, yanked his towel off his hips, and wiped his face.

"Jesus." Nic spun and left the bathroom.

"You're the one who came in for a show. Take it like a man." Percy laughed, and it was the first time in days he'd heard it. Damn, he'd screwed up with everyone around here. "Get the driver while I get dressed. Sasha's only minutes away."

"You knew where he was?"

"Of course. I was his only friend here."

The words seared like acid. He'd let Sasha down in so many ways. How could he ever make up for that? Maybe he wouldn't want anything to do with Nic again. If so, Nic didn't care how long it took. He'd win him back.

"Wait," Percy called right before entering the bedroom. "It's late. You might do better with a plan."

"Like what?"

"You know, surprise him with something nice. Breakfast, flowers, chocolate, a new car. I don't know. Whatever floats your boat."

"I doubt he could be bought, Percy."

His friend sighed heavily. "I feel sorry for Sasha getting you as a boyfriend. At least look like you put in some effort for him. Shit, Nic, you were an asshole of the biggest variety."

Yeah, of course. Why didn't he think of that? "You're right," he said. Percy nodded. "I'll think of something, but be ready early. I'm not very patient."

"I think we all know that. Now get the hell out of my room."

Nic went to his own master suite where he stayed up for hours thinking about what he should say and do, how Sasha might react, whether he'd lost him for good. There was no one on the planet like Sasha, and he wasn't going to walk away again.

Chapter Eighteen

Sasha

LEANING over the sink, Sasha rubbed the scruff on his chin, considered shaving it, and discarded the idea. What did he have to get dressed up for anyway? With a little over a week until Christmas, there weren't a lot of teaching positions available to apply for, and the few interviews he'd picked up weren't scheduled until after the school break.

He crossed the room to his tiny kitchen table to sit, tipped his chair back, and kicked his feet up onto the corner of the table. The bottle of Jack beckoned, and he answered its call. Eight in the morning? That wasn't too early when your life had suddenly emptied like a sailor's wallet in a liberty port. A laugh that sounded too close to a sob escaped him as he tipped the bottle back.

Most of his life, he'd been the motivational guy, the fun-times guy, the silver-linings guy, the one to lift others up even when he hadn't felt any of it, even at the worst of times. Hope had been what he'd pulled it all from, wanting to believe happiness waited at the end of the battle as long as there was no giving in. That was over now. Something inside him didn't work anymore.

Once, he'd had a remote control with a broken piece inside that rattled and made the volume stick. He was the same, his emotional volume set to one level, maybe forever, with everything dull, muted, gray. Smiling was so out of his reach these days, he couldn't even fake one anymore.

All his life, no matter where in the world his parents had gone, Sasha had loved Christmas and everything about the season, even though he'd mostly been alone. It never failed to lift him into another world where wishes came true, good people outnumbered the bad, everything was beautiful, and the spirit of giving prevailed. The past few days, he'd tried so hard to get that feeling back, the excitement, the fun. *Fucking broken volume button.* So much for picking himself back up.

He'd been staring off into space for countless minutes when a knock came at the door. His first urge was to ignore it. No one but Percy knew where he was, so it was probably someone soliciting. Girl Scout cookie season hadn't started yet. The knock came again. What the hell, why not? Mormon missionaries could be damned cute, and there was no doubt his loneliness was about to swallow him whole.

Without bothering with a shirt, he pulled the door open and froze in midgreeting. Nic stood at his door with his hand raised to knock again. Dammit, why'd the man have to look so good? Even with exhaustion layered over his handsome features, he was the kind of sexy that seemed unreal, the kind that drew stares, and it hurt to look at him. Who was he kidding? Everything hurt right now.

"Hi." Nic's voice was barely above a whisper. He dropped his hand and gestured toward the studio's interior. "Can I come in?"

Some petty part of Sasha wanted to shut the door in his face, but instead he took a step back. "Uh, sure."

Sasha hadn't noticed the large basket until Nic picked it up from where it sat next to him. He brought it in and placed it on the table, which was so small, the basket nearly covered its surface. Nic took a second to look around while Sasha closed the door. Yeah, it *would* only take a second. The place was a hole in the wall, barely a studio, with a tiny room in the corner where the toilet and shower stall were. Even the bathroom sink and mirror were in the single main room. And worse, Sasha didn't have proper furniture, having left everything with Drew back in California. A bare mattress propped up on milk crates sat in the corner of the room. At least that was neatly made up with decent bedding.

Sasha had never cared about how cramped and plain the room was until Nic was here. Now he shifted uncomfortably, waiting for Nic to pass judgment. When he didn't say anything, Sasha dropped back into his seat, surreptitiously glancing at the bottle of JD next to the basket. Shit. As if his living situation weren't embarrassing enough. Couldn't he have at least used a glass?

Nic opened the basket and unpacked a few things, some wrapped breakfast sandwiches, fruit, fresh coffee. "I brought breakfast."

Sasha shrugged. "I'm not hungry."

With a sigh, Nic's eyes trailed down his bare chest, and Sasha knew what he was seeing. So, yeah, he'd lost a little weight over the past week, but he wasn't starving or anything. Nothing sounded good. Even when he had hunger pangs, he didn't have an appetite.

To his utter shock, Nic dropped to his knees in front of Sasha's chair and took Sasha's hands, the intensity in Nic's expression taking his breath away. "I'm so sorry," Nic rasped. "So fucking sorry, Sasha. I fucked up. I got scared. Everything started unraveling, all my work falling apart, and it was easier to push you away and blame you. None of it was your fault."

Those emerald eyes searched Sasha's face, but he wasn't sure what to say to that. His heart pounded out a hard rhythm, and heat warmed his cold body for the first time in days, but that broken thing in him was a weight holding him down. He wanted to be happy that Nic seemed to have changed his mind, but wanting happiness and being happy were very different beasts.

"Please, come back, Sasha."

He pulled his hands from Nic's, stood up, and paced between the table and the foot of his makeshift bed. His gut cried out to go back home—*hah, home*. Like it had ever been his. Yet in the month he'd lived there, it had felt more like home than his own childhood house.

"I can't." He turned to Nic, who'd risen to his feet. The pain on Nic's face doubled the pain in Sasha's chest. Nic actually felt something for him, then. Maybe this wasn't a ploy, another shaky employment offer. "Nic, I can't work for someone I have feelings for, someone I have a relationship with. Because look what happens." He gestured around the room.

Something took over Nic's expression, a burst of surprise mixed with a bit of wonder. His brows rose, and he moved right into Sasha's space, nearly chest to chest. Sasha's breathing sped up.

"Do you, Sasha?" he asked, holding Sasha's gaze, his lips hovering only an inch away so his warm, minty breath puffed against Sasha's. "Do you feel for me? You want a relationship with me?"

Sasha barely nodded before Nic's hands cradled his head, holding him fast for a devouring kiss. And another and another. Nic kissed him over and over, deep, slow, heady kisses, pressing his body into Sasha's. That passion and sincerity eroded Sasha's meager resistance. Nic pulled back, out of breath, before leaning his forehead against Sasha's, his eyes burning with emotion.

"I want this, a relationship with you. I love you, Sasha," he said. "Yeah, I want you to come home, but if you need to be here, I can live with it as long as we're together."

Taking a chance on Nic was risky. They'd only been around each other a few weeks. What would happen next time Nic freaked out and Sasha was even more in love than he was now? It would destroy him, maybe permanently. With a small shake of his head, Sasha started to take a step back, but Nic grabbed his hips and jerked him close.

"Don't," he said. "Sasha, don't make the same mistake I did out of fear. If you want me, take me. I'm yours."

An almost-whimper came out of Sasha, and it lit Nic's eyes with fire. He wrapped his arms around Sasha, his hands tracing Sasha's spine, pressing into the muscles. Sasha's thoughts scattered, his focus blown. Working his way along Sasha's jaw and throat, Nic sucked and licked, leaving hot patches that would end up as red marks and wrecking Sasha's resistance even further. Not much felt more incredible than Nic's mouth on Sasha's body, especially his throat. Sasha moaned his pleasure and couldn't stop grinding his hips against Nic.

"That feel good, Sasha?" he whispered between kisses. "Wanna get my clothes off?"

Another tremulous moan, and then Sasha fumbled with Nic's buttons until he couldn't wait anymore. He popped the last few and peeled the shirt from those broad shoulders, running his shaking hands along Nic's lean muscles as he went. Then Nic caught them against his chest.

"Sasha?"

Sasha waited, but Nic didn't say anything more for several minutes. Maybe he sensed the knot of discord driving Sasha, making him so fucking frantic. The destructive force of their sudden breakup remained inside Sasha, a malicious echo whispering how alone he was no matter what Nic said. Getting physical with Nic was a way to ease those whispers, to be connected to his lover again. He could convince himself for a while that making love was the same as having love.

It wasn't, though, and somehow, Nic knew better. He released one of Sasha's hands and tugged him down to lie on the bed. He continued to pet Sasha, tracing his face and pushing through his hair. Finally, Nic leaned over to press his lips against Sasha's ear. "I'm so sorry I hurt you, and I'll never say that enough. I love you."

He wanted to believe him, but he was still raw with the pain of the last few days. He rolled over to see Nic's face, and Nic propped himself up on his elbow, bending down to kiss Sasha's lips. Nic tucked his face against Sasha's throat and wrapped his free arm tightly around him.

"You've only known me a few weeks."

"I know. Why do you think I got gun shy?" Nic shrugged one muscular shoulder. "We kind of went from zero to sixty in a few days."

Sasha hesitated, running his fingers through Nic's trim, dark chest hair. "I don't want you to think I don't feel the same, because I do. What you did wouldn't have hurt so much if I didn't." Nic cringed, his eyes closing, and Sasha almost regretted bringing it up. "But we haven't even been on a date. We're all backward."

Surprisingly, Nic opened his eyes and laughed. If Sasha hadn't been lying down, the affection in those gorgeous green eyes might have knocked him on his ass. "I'm not worried. All my friends started out either fucking or rooming together before ever dating properly. Look at us. We did both."

"Meh. I'm not admitting even a little that you might have a point. The couples I know dated first."

"Grindr meetups don't count as dating."

"Why not? It's a dating app."

"You mean hookup app. Most people ditch the date before it happens or hook up."

"Overgeneralizing, sir."

"Yes, I am." Nic nodded and then grinned. "I kind of like that too much, you calling me sir."

He gave Nic a slight shove. "Well, don't get used to it, asshole. I'm a bottom, not a sub."

With a happy-sounding grunt, Nic hopped off the bed and pulled his shirt back on before grabbing a sandwich and some ripe berries from the table and climbing back on the bed, sitting on it crossways to lean against the wall. He pulled Sasha up beside him.

"Here." He pushed a hulled strawberry between Sasha's lips. "I need to feed you. Humor me, would you?"

Sasha shrugged and ate the berry. It was bursting with a perfect balance of sweet and tart. "Where'd you find good berries in the middle of December?"

"Hothouses. I had Vicki source them last night." He shook his head as he fed Sasha another berry. "She was *not* happy when I called."

He could imagine the picky chef's annoyed face. Again, Sasha wanted to laugh but couldn't, only managing a weak smile before chewing his strawberry. "That was some effort. To woo me, huh?"

"Yep, but it was a few other people's effort. I was just ready to beg, maybe camp outside your door."

"Gah, you're telling me this now?" Sasha tugged Nic's arm. "Go back outside. We'll start over, and I'll hold out longer."

"Nope. Too late for take backs. I'll beg and grovel some other time if it'll make you happy." He paused and cupped Sasha's jaw, a frown and creased brow settling on his features. "You're still hurt," he whispered and then sucked in a sharp breath at whatever he saw in Sasha's eyes. "I *hate* what I've done to you. I promise, Sasha, I'll heal this between us no matter how long it takes."

"Nic, it's okay. You're here now. You apologized." None of the worry left Nic's face, so Sasha continued. "And I accept it. Your apology. All right? I'm sorry, too, that—"

"You did nothing wrong that needs an apology."

"Well, I'm sorry anyway." Sasha took the breakfast sandwich Nic shoved at him and ate a bite before explaining. "I mean, sorry things went to shit at work. I don't regret last Sunday because it was the best day of my life, but I'm sorry about after."

They ate in silence the next few minutes before Nic cleared his throat. "The kids miss you desperately.

Any idea how often you want to come over? They're on break now until the New Year."

There was a hopeful light in Nic's eyes, and it drove guilt through Sasha's stomach, making it impossible to force any more food down.

"Maybe we could have a game night tomorrow," Sasha said.

"I'll never think of a game night or movie night the same again." Nic grinned and then frowned. He pulled Sasha into his lap and hugged him so hard, he could barely draw a breath. "All right. Tomorrow night. Have dinner with us around five, okay?" He waited to feel Sasha's nod, and then his hands rubbed Sasha's back. It felt so good, Sasha nearly purred. When Nic finally withdrew, it was slowly and with great reluctance, but he said he had work to wrap up so he'd have more free time over the break.

Hmm, imagine Nic trying to make free time. Obviously, Nic's priorities had shifted, which was a great thing, especially for Lucy and Ben, who Sasha missed like crazy. He couldn't wait to see them tomorrow, even though it might not show much outwardly. By the time Nic left with a final kiss and insisting Sasha eat the rest of the food, that worry hadn't left Nic's expression.

It was clear Nic sensed the wounds still open in him, but Nic's rejection had only been the last straw, the one that broke him. Nic's apology, his loving words and his touch, helped soothe the deepest ache, but the sharp edges of his memories still drew blood. He wanted so much to go back to the way he felt that last weekend before his world fell apart, and it was, no doubt, why he'd offered little resistance to Nic. Or was he falling into the same old patterns again? Would he repeatedly give in to Nic to keep up the façade of being agreeable?

Hey, look at me. I'm a good boy. I promise I won't cause trouble. Please, keep me this time.

If only there were a humane society for lonely boys who get thrown away. He slumped back onto his bed, ignoring the strawberries he spilled over the bedspread. If things were going to work out with Nic, he had to find a way to toss those old patterns and be a real partner. But would Nic still want him if he knew the whole Sasha, drama and all? It would mean trusting Nic more than ever, the one thing he wasn't ready to do after the past few days. As if his love troubles weren't enough, getting his budding relationship back with Nic wasn't going to magically fix everything else wrong in Sasha's life. Maybe once Sasha put everything else right, he could fix that broken thing and be himself once more.

But sometimes what was broken never went back the same way again.

Chapter Nineteen

Nic

FOUR days. After getting Sasha back, he should've been bursting with joy like he never had in his life. Oh yeah, he was bursting sure enough, but it wasn't joy filling him. It was heaps of frustration, a touch of anxiety, and a dash of confusion. He'd spent many hours each of these past four days with Sasha, in and out of bed, and they were all good hours. Yet an insurmountable wall surrounded him, one that even Lucy and Ben couldn't get through.

The office phone rang, making him flinch and yanking him from his thoughts. Who the heck would call him on the landline? When he picked it up, he was surprised to hear Ben's voice on the line.

"Family meeting," Ben said. No greeting, no explanation, and no request. Just a demand. "In the den." Then, he hung up on Nic. It was too early for this crap, and he needed to get to work. Nic shoved out of his chair, tossed his jacket on, grabbed the reports he was preparing for the board meeting later, and headed to the den. Lucy and Ben were already seated, and Percy walked in at the same time as Nic, both taking the sofa across from the kids.

"Your uncle and I need to get to work soon. Big board meeting today," Percy said, reading Nic's thoughts as usual. "What's on your mind?"

"This won't take long." Lucy sat forward and flipped her long curly hair over her shoulder and out of her face. "We're worried about Sasha."

"Something's wrong with Sasha," Ben said at the same time. They looked at each other for a moment, and then Lucy continued.

"He never laughs anymore, and his smiles aren't real." She narrowed her eyes at Nic. "Did you apologize enough last Sunday? Are you being good to him?"

Nic threw his arms out. "Christ's sake, Lucy, you've seen us together. I love the heck out of that man. I'd cut myself open and lay my guts out for him if he asked."

"Ew, gross."

"Coooool."

"Kids," Percy said, including Nic in his scowl. "As much as I'd *love* to see that disembowelment, I don't think Nic is why Sasha's down lately."

Nic straightened in his seat. "I ask him sometimes, but he always says he's fine. Okay, then it's not only me seeing this."

"No," Lucy said. "But this started with the breakup. You're back with him, so what else has changed since then?"

"He's not living here anymore." Ben was focused on the floor as he spoke. Yes, Nic was disappointed about that fact, but it sounded like Ben had been upset about it too.

"I tried," Nic explained. "A few times actually. He wouldn't move back."

Percy grunted. "Doesn't want to be dependent."

"What?" Dependent? But Nic had even offered to *rent* him a room the other day, trying like some desperate stalker to keep Sasha closer.

"Maybe it's his job. We all know what stress at work can do to a person." Lucy looked pointedly at Nic.

He snorted. "Wait till it's you." He thought back all the way to Sunday. "He never mentioned work."

"It means he hasn't found anything yet."

Nic eyed Percy. "Then how's he paying for his apartment? Or his bills or gas and food?"

Shoving back in his seat, Percy leaned his head on the cushion behind him. "When he left, Sasha had no money and nowhere to go." His words shoved a spike through Nic's heart, and Percy seemed to know it, turning his head to meet Nic's eyes. "Stop beating yourself up, Nic. I wasn't trying to guilt you. I just meant he was in a bad place, but he wouldn't accept any money, not even a loan. Trust me, I offered. The only thing that worked was helping him sell his truck."

Shock punched through Nic's body. How had he not noticed Sasha hadn't been driving his truck? "What the fuck, Percy? He loved that truck."

"And it's the only thing he had with any equity left." He shot Nic a glare. "I was trying to help him, dickhead. It was high value, but he only had a few grand of equity. It was enough to cover the move-in costs and get him by for a month or so. I gave him a recommendation to get a substitute position with hiring potential at Vashon schools. Obviously, there's no work for him for a while because of the holiday."

"Why wouldn't he tell me any of this? If he's struggling, why wouldn't he say anything? I'm in a perfect position to help him."

"Uncle Nic, have you met Sasha?" Ben rolled his eyes. "He doesn't talk problems unless they're someone else's. I always thought he was the cheeriest person on Earth. Then I heard him on the phone with his dad on Thanksgiving. After that, I didn't give him such a hard time anymore."

Lucy smacked his arm. "You shouldn't have been a butthead to begin with."

"Hah, like you were any better when he first got here."

Sasha had told him a little, letting Nic in more than he apparently let most people in. And what had Nic done? Abandoned him when things got tough, as his parents had time and again.

"Damn. I guess that explains a lot." Percy sighed heavily, and when he looked up, guilt flashed across his face. "He asked why you didn't call him yourself, and I said you had enough problems to deal with."

"*Fuck.*" Before Nic could stop it, a sound like some wounded animal left his throat. He leaped up and paced at the end of the sofas, his hands running through his hair. "He'll never believe me. I have to show him."

"Show him what?" Lucy asked, but Nic didn't answer. "Uncle Nic! Show him what?"

He turned to his family. "Show him I can handle it, all of it. The good, the bad, the ugly. Quick. We don't have much time. I have to get to this damn board meeting, but Percy, I have things for you to do while I'm in there."

"You sure you don't need moral support?" Percy asked. "Your father's going to be there."

Nic shook his head. "This is more important."

Everyone stared at him with mouths agape and eyebrows raised. Was it that out of character for him to put something before the business? It's not like he hadn't put them first when he could. Right? He frowned. Hadn't he? When he thought back, it had always been Percy or a nanny or caregiver going to the kids' schools when they had trouble or extracurricular activities. He'd missed every holiday with the kids since last New Year's.

And Percy? He couldn't remember the last time he'd gone out for drinks with Percy when it wasn't a business trip. They used to go camping, sailing, and scuba diving all the time before Nic's father had retired from his CEO seat. Shit, he didn't know about anything going on in Percy's life lately. Was he dating someone new after his ex-boyfriend had gotten him all twisted up nearly a year ago? Nic had to have been blind all this time. After all, he lived in the same damn house with Percy. What a shitty friend he was turning out to be.

"Anyway, it's time to go. The helo's on standby." He leaned down to hug each of the kids. Even the hugs had been something Sasha had brought back into Nic's life. "Don't worry. I'm going to do everything I can to help Sasha."

As he and Percy headed into the office, Nic gave Percy instructions on what needed to be done. He needed to review his reports for the meeting, but he couldn't concentrate on anything except his forthcoming conversation with Sasha.

When they arrived, the board was getting ready to convene, and Nic parted ways with Percy. He entered the smaller conference room. All ten members of the board, including his father, were already seated and well into their coffee and pastries. Well, this was confusing. He was nearly ten minutes early, so why were they all here as if they'd agreed to an earlier time, leaving him out of the loop?

"Nicolas, have a seat." His father gestured toward Nic's normal position at the end of the conference table.

Nic lifted his brows but sat as directed, dropping his reports on the table in front of him. "Well, hello. Everyone's here early. Was I-5 traffic decent today or did someone change the meeting schedule?"

A few people suppressed laughter, but most of the members' faces remained serious. This didn't bode well. Maybe he'd gotten the time wrong. His father stood at the head of the table, surveyed all the board members, giving a couple of them stern looks, and finally settled his gaze on Nic.

"We've conducted a meeting early this morning, so this one is a special convening of the board," he said.

"You had one without your CEO present?" Nic asked, panning the room not much differently than his father had a moment earlier. Most of the members wouldn't make eye contact with Nic.

"In light of the decline over the last few quarters and the recent lawsuit—"

"Which was resolved, dropped by the plaintiff."

"And the contracts that were lost—"

"Which were all recovered or replaced with an actual increase in sales."

His father cleared his throat, his face turning a somewhat dark shade of pink. "We, the board, have decided to relieve you of your position as CEO. The vote was unanimous." Several members, ones who couldn't make eye contact earlier, squirmed in their seats. "The search for a replacement CEO will begin immediately with planned turnover set for the end of February."

His father kept talking through all the formalities, severance package details, hiring process for the replacement, and so on, but Nic had checked out. He was supposed to have until the end of the quarter to pick up the numbers. He was supposed to have more time. He'd still met their demands, even considering the quarter wasn't over. Yet they'd still fired him, and in an underhanded way, as if he'd done something wrong.

Numbness slid through him, beginning with his limbs and then his face and finally his chest. A floating sensation like he'd been set adrift pushed at the top of his head and dizziness crept in. *Anxiety.* This place was all he'd known, and it had consumed his life. What would he do now?

He'd never had a chance. His parents had already decided months ago to replace Nic. They talked about giving him the quarter, but here it was the most successful quarter in nearly a year and he was still getting canned. After a decade of dedication and sacrifice at his own family business.

He looked around at the board members. Most of them he liked and respected. He couldn't even hold this against them. Nic's father was a controlling stockholder along with Nic's mother. If his father decided to get rid of a CEO, there was no override. If members voted against him, he could have them removed from the board. No one could even fight for Nic, including himself.

Sasha's words echoed in his thoughts. *Would it be such a bad thing to try something new?* He'd had faith that

Nic would succeed without Leighton Price, that he could be happy somewhere else, maybe with the expansion proposed by Basile. Would he have had the strength to go for the deal if not for Sasha? The opportunity in the first place might never have come without him. If not for the Christmas cookie baking incident. Somehow, that man's faith in him dragged Nic back from the edge, reassured him that he could remain standing despite this blow.

"We'll need the new contracts completed and the quarterly rep—"

Nic rose from his seat and gathered his reports.

"Nicolas, are you listening? Where are you going?"

He faced the board members. "It's been wonderful working with you all. Some of you I've worked with from the time I first arrived fresh from my MBA, and you've given me valuable advice and guidance. I'll miss having that in whatever venture I take on next. Despite these unfortunate circumstances, I do wish you all well. Have a wonderful day."

He'd reached the door by the time his flustered father could say anything. "Are you leaving? You can't leave right now. We're not finished."

"Yes, I believe we are," Nic said, pausing at the door. "I'm due over forty days of paid leave. I believe that takes me all the way out to my termination date. My lawyer will work with HR on the severance package while I'm on leave. I believe that about covers it. Oh, well, except for my staff. They'll be coming with me. Both Summer and Percy will be submitting their resignations today as well. As they don't have employment contracts, their resignations will be in HR before the day's over."

Okay, so he probably should have consulted Summer, but if he'd doubted his secretary would come with him, he wouldn't have mentioned her. Percy was an easy bet. The only reason his friend had stayed at Leighton Price this long was that he would never see Nic if they didn't work together.

"You can't quit without notice!" His father had completely lost his composure for once, scowling heavily with his voice raised.

"I didn't resign. I was terminated with a unanimous vote by the board of directors. You may state whatever date you wish, but my employment contract stipulates thirty days after the vote as the termination date. My contract-guaranteed leave more than covers all of those thirty days. The paperwork is going to HR today, and my leave begins tomorrow. I wish you luck in your hunt for a competent CEO."

He didn't give his father a chance at another word. Nic left for his office. Summer wasn't upset when Nic explained things to her, but she was nervous about lapses in pay. Once he assured her she wouldn't have to move and he'd cover everything and even send her on a paid vacation until he'd transitioned to the new company, she was excited about it.

Several hours later, an unbelievably high stack of paperwork had been completed, and Nic had made the call to Anselmo to broker the business meeting between his in-laws and Nic. Anselmo was ecstatic about Nic's decision to partner with the family.

Soon after, Nic, accompanied by Percy, was on the helo crossing the Sound. He began to laugh, and he couldn't stop, even when Percy looked at him like he was an escaped mental patient. He was free as he'd never been before, with no expectations to meet but his own. A lightness of being struck him, and there was nothing he wanted more than for Sasha to feel it. This had to be what happiness felt like. Had he ever felt it fully until now?

"All right, who are you and what have you done with my best friend?" Percy asked as they left the helo.

A wide smile stuck on his face, Nic threw an arm over Percy's shoulder. "I guess this is what happens when you find out the tumor is gone. How about you? How are you doing with being jobless and all?"

Giving in, Percy laughed. "Are you trying to tell me that being your friend isn't work?"

"I've been paying you? I need a new accountant, then," Nic said. His smile faltered slightly. "Please tell me you were able to do what I needed to be done today."

"No worries. It's done."

Nic nodded. "Thank you."

"Not sure you'll want to thank me yet." A grimace crossed Percy's face. "I think you'll have your work cut out for you trying to convince Sasha to dump on you without dumping your dumb ass."

"He kind of has no choice. There's not a feasible way to reverse what I had you do."

"Which is why I say, 'You only live dangerously once.'"

As they entered the first-floor foyer, Nic pointed toward the rear where Percy's suite was. "Go to your room and stay away from me. Your negativity might be contagious."

Percy started to do just that but then stopped. "Hey, Nic. It's good to see you this way. I haven't seen you like this since we were in college."

Nic's gaze followed Percy until he disappeared down the hall. Yeah, he remembered those days, too, his first taste of freedom. It had been good until his father had yanked the familial leash. He'd had no resources of his own, attending on scholarships and his parents' money. The family business had never been something he'd wanted, only something expected and then demanded as payment for Nic's education.

Things were different now. Nic had his own money, billions, and his own resources. His house was his own, his assets, his helicopter—all his and acquired through hard work, conservative management, and smart investments. His work ethic had earned valuable contacts in the business world, and that was the best thing he'd ever gained from Leighton Price. Yes, he probably could have gotten a decent position somewhere on his own, but surviving and thriving weren't the same.

He was going to thrive because of Sasha, and he damned well had to make sure Sasha thrived too. With Nic. If that meant taking on every little battle Sasha had ever fought alone, he would demand it. Earlier, Sasha had called but said he had business to take care of and wouldn't be over. So tonight, Nic would be patient and wait until tomorrow. But tomorrow was another story. He'd go to Sasha's and wouldn't leave until he had full access to every one of Sasha's problems. Tomorrow, he wanted trouble.

Chapter Twenty

Sasha

SASHA braced against the wall and bent over at the waist, clutching his stomach and suspecting he might be getting an ulcer. On top of the sharp physical pain, he was exhausted. Yesterday, it had taken all morning to get to Seattle for an interview he'd picked up at the last minute and most of the afternoon to get back home. He should have invested in a bike, but that purchase, as small as it was, would've pushed his finances.

Even in the fairly enlightened Pacific Northwest, people were wary of males working with children—and not completely without reason—so he hadn't been able to get temporary work as a caregiver. Tutoring wasn't an option during the holidays, the demand for people with math degrees was laughable, and lifeguarding was a summertime thing. At this rate, he could end up flipping burgers until school started again.

A college kid had better prospects than he did. That led Sasha right back to the decisions eating him alive. Acquiring a low-interest loan was out of the question with no job and a high debt-to-income ratio. Predatory were the only ones left, and he didn't have the means to pay the high-interest costs. He had nothing left to sell except blood plasma, but his skin crawled at the mere thought of the huge needles.

It wasn't only money eating him. His entire life dangled in a void of uncertainty, leaving him aimless. Taking care of Lucy and Ben had been more rewarding than he could have imagined, but his life's dream had always been to teach. He thought he'd found his place in California, but his disastrous relationship with Drew had killed that fantasy. Home, family, career, all of it had become so far out of his reach. He sank to the floor, his back to the wall and head in his hands. The ache in his throat grew as he fought to curb his spiraling desolation. What would it take to set his life upright again? If he ever did. He wasn't doing recovery too well these days.

In some ways, spending time with Nic and the kids took pressure off him, but it hovered at the back of his mind, waiting to pounce on him at every quiet moment. With only four more days until Christmas, the pressure was growing. He wanted to do something special for the kids, Percy, and especially for Nic, but his financial situation made everything so tight, the idea of Christmas was practically choking him. For the first time, he understood why Christmas was the worst time of year for many people.

It took a few seconds before he noticed the knocking on his door.

"Sasha?" Nic's voice sang through him, sending his heart soaring. "Time to get up, sunshine."

He groaned as he stood, muscles sore like he was eighty instead of nearly thirty. "Coming. Hold your damned horses."

When Nic came in, he was so fucking handsome, Sasha couldn't keep his eyes off him. He wore a deep red button-up with a light pattern of tiny diamonds and midnight blue stressed denim jeans. In his hand, he held a folder that he flicked back and forth against his thigh.

"Wow," Sasha said, sliding his palms over Nic's hips. "It's early on a weekday, and you're not at work. Did hell freeze over or something?"

Instead of answering, Nic clasped the nape of Sasha's neck with his free hand and dipped in for a nearly ferocious kiss. His tongue pushed beyond Sasha's lips to trace his teeth, the inside of his cheeks, the roof of his mouth, gliding along his tongue and then sucking it lightly before releasing Sasha. The pressure of Nic's mouth left Sasha's lips tingling.

"Not exactly." Nic lowered his forehead to Sasha's, a smile lighting up his face. Even his eyes brightened with it. "But I'm free of it. Free of hell, I mean. I lost my job today."

Sasha drew back, frowning. "What? Why? And you're happy?"

Nic laughed. "Absolutely. I've never felt better."

He studied Nic's face and a zing of disbelief went through him. "You really are. That's amazing. What will you do now? What about your parents?"

Grumbling, Nic tugged Sasha over to the table where he tossed the file, sat down, and pulled Sasha into his lap.

"My parents are the ones who fired me, so I don't much care how they're feeling. Now, my plans, on the other hand, I care about very much. I've never been so excited about a venture, and I owe you for all of it."

Sasha raised his brows, loving the way Nic was stroking his thigh while he spoke, his other hand running through Sasha's hair.

"How's that? All I've done was take care of the kids."

"You sealed the deal with the De Francos, and then you gave me the confidence to take that partnership with their in-laws, the one I told you about a couple weeks ago." Sasha shook his head, but Nic gripped his hair tightly. "Don't negate what you did."

"I'm not. I don't think anything I did was as big a deal as all that." Sasha stood, grabbing a beer from the fridge. "Want one?"

"No. I want you to talk to me."

Sasha sat across from Nic and downed a chug of beer. "I'm talking."

"But you aren't, Sasha." Leaning forward, Nic took his hand. "You're keeping everything inside. Do you think I can't see you're stressed out? We all see how much it's affecting you."

He sighed and tried to sit back, but Nic held him fast. Part of him wanted to spill everything to Nic— really, really wanted to spill. Then, history tightened a band around his chest, making it impossible to slip a word out.

Nic cupped Sasha's jaw, and his voice was as tender and full of affection as his gaze. "I know how you grew up and how people in your past have treated you. You're trying not to cause trouble or be trouble. I get that, but I want all of you, Sasha, every little bit. I want to know what's stressing you out, what's hurting you. I want to know all your problems, everything weighing you down, and I want to help you carry that weight."

He launched out of his seat, jerking away from Nic's touch. Dread stabbed through the middle of him, making his stomach cramp again, nearly doubling him over. Nic seemed sincere, but Sasha had been through this many times before. People asked if someone was okay, but they never wanted to hear about when they weren't. Any response other than "I'm fine" was unwelcome, uncomfortable.

Nic, as much as Sasha loved him, wouldn't be different. He'd eventually resent Sasha's dependence on him, especially now, when Sasha would be so fucking needy if he caved in to his urge to confide in someone—anyone.

"Don't hide yourself from me." Nic rose to face Sasha.

"Look, if I'm having personal issues, it's not your duty to fix them."

"That's where we disagree." He moved closer to Sasha, but all that did was ramp up Sasha's fear.

"You sent me away because I was a problem for you. So no, Nic, I'm not going to dump my shit on you. Please, stop asking me."

"You haven't forgiven me, have you?"

He nodded, his eyes dropping to Nic's chest. "I have."

"Stop it, Sasha. I fucked everything up. When everything went to hell, I ran away like a coward." A sudden realization spread over Nic's expression. "And it was so damned easy to get you back. Why?"

Sasha tried to turn away, but Nic caught his shoulders.

"Why didn't you give me shit?" When Sasha tried to pull away again, Nic held fast. "You didn't want to upset me, did you? Fuck's sake, please tell me that's not what happened."

"I don't want to talk about this." His blood pressure spiked, his pulse racing as the thoughts and feelings from that day churned back up.

"I'm not leaving here until we work all this out. Aren't you angry? I fired you. I kicked you out. Aren't you furious, Sasha? I forced you away from the kids. What are you feeling about all this? I dumped you, left you without so much as a—"

"Yes, I'm fucking pissed off! Okay? Is that what you want to hear?" He shoved Nic's chest, his head pounding and his eyes burning. "I didn't do *anything* to you, and you blamed me for *everything*. You used me and threw me away like I was nothing to you. How could you?"

He shoved Nic again and then again and again with each choked sentence. "Couldn't even look me in the face. What kind of man does that to a person? I had *nothing* left. Why would you do this to me? I fucking loved you, and you hurt me. It fucking hurts."

His knees buckled, but Nic caught him, surrounded him with his arms, and lowered him to the edge of the mattress. Sasha couldn't stop shaking, his ears ringing so loudly it took a while to hear Nic murmuring in his ear as he held him.

"…make everything right because I love you so much. I'll never let anything happen to you. I need you in my life, and I want to take care of you. I want to know everything that hurts you, every problem you're facing. You're going to be happy again. I'll make sure. Nothing you say will ever make me leave you again."

Sasha closed his eyes and let the words wash over him, calming his heart rate and easing the tightness in his chest. Then, regret struck him. He really thought he'd been over his rejection. "I'm sorry. I can't—"

"Sasha." Nic pressed him flat on his back on the bed and gazed deeply into his eyes. "I'm not like Drew, and I'm nothing like your parents. When you've got shit to work through, you can talk to me. You can tell me when you're upset or angry or sad. I've spent years running a billion-dollar corporation. Conflict, challenges, problems—whatever you'd call them—are just another item on the agenda, so go ahead. Get in my face, get pissed, rant at me. I'm strong enough to handle it."

He groaned. "I don't want to bring anyone down, especially this time of year."

"Oh, babe," Nic said. "Listen to me. You are the best man I've ever known, and you make me a better man. You could never bring any of us down. And that's why I've paid off that stupid mortgage hanging around your throat."

"You did what?"

"I paid that fucker off yesterday, and I knew it would upset you because you're worried about how I'd look at you afterward. I paid it anyway because the money means nothing to me, not even the slightest. But getting that off your shoulders means everything to you, and *doing that* means everything to me."

Some subconscious tether inside him gave way, and the strange floating sensation he'd had before returned, only this time, it didn't arrive with anxiety and dizziness. It brought nothing but warmth with it, and then he could breathe as if he'd never truly been breathing before.

"Sasha, I did something else," Nic continued, still watching his face closely. "I found a position open for an upper-class math teacher at Lakeside School in Seattle. I realize it's a private school, but they have a math team that goes everywhere for competitions." Nic grinned at whatever he saw on Sasha's face. "God, I love seeing that excitement in your eyes again, but who the fuck gets excited about math?"

Sasha laughed. He sure as shit laughed. It'd been nearly two weeks since he'd last done that. "I can teach you to get excited about math." Then, he frowned. "But Nic—"

"Don't argue this time, you stubborn ass. I did this for you with Percy's help, and not only will you accept it, but you're going to give me more, starting with your damned student loans. Then, you *will* move in with me, even if it's to your old suite in the house. Then, in case you're worried about a commute when you nail this job application process, you *will* use the helo and one of the drivers to get there."

Nic brushed his nose against Sasha's. "You're going to let me do all of it. I want to. I need to do it. We're together now, Sasha, and that means carrying our burdens together too."

Tipping his head back on the bedspread and closing his eyes, Sasha relaxed, and his headache finally eased up. "I can tell you anything that's bothering me?"

"God yes. Please."

His gaze whipped over to Nic and read the resolve on that handsome face. It was true, undeniably true. Nic wanted this from him. Disbelief hit him again, followed by that warm feeling spreading through his limbs.

"I abhor the decorations in the house," he admitted grudgingly. "When I'm there sometimes, I feel like I'm in a Macy's or something."

Nic only grinned—no superior disapproval, no huffs of indignation, no righteous anger, just a stupidly happy grin. "You know, they've never bothered me before, but after the past few weeks, I've been feeling the same way. And it's never been a secret how much the kids hate them. Let's take them down this weekend and put up new ones. You still have the ones you had up when I first got here after Thanksgiving?"

He nodded and then, to his disgust, the tears he'd fought back earlier stung his eyes and then pooled in them.

Nic moved on top of Sasha and cradled Sasha's head with his hands. "It's okay, Sasha. Whatever you feel, I won't turn away. When you're with me, you can let go because I'll keep you safe." He shook his head. "You have no idea what you've done for me. If not for you, I never would have remembered who I was without my parents' voices in my head. Nothing you do or say would make me love you less."

Nothing had ever sounded better, and nothing felt better than having someone care for him. He pulled Nic's head down so he could kiss him, and then they couldn't stop. It didn't help that Nic lay between Sasha's thighs and started grinding against him.

"I swear," Nic whispered between kisses, "I didn't mean for this to be a seduction."

Sasha bit Nic's lower lip. "It's not one if I seduce you first." Then he drew back. "I'm not comfortable accepting money from you."

"I know." Nic blew out a sigh. "That's your pride talking. We need to find a way around that because I want to take care of you without it creating inequity between us. You already said you didn't want to work for me."

"Yeah, that didn't turn out so well for me before."

"Sasha, I'd never—"

"I know you wouldn't. More than ever, I know. Right now, I think I can wait until after school starts before I need to panic about a job. Somehow, my debt is suddenly gone." He grinned at those words, the truth of them finally beginning to sink in fully.

Nuzzling Sasha's neck, Nic began trailing kisses downward, speaking between them. "You're killing me. I'm trying not to pressure you, but I want you home so badly, I'm willing to do anything. If I can't hire you, what can I do? I don't want to have Christmas without you. None of us do. The kids need you. I need you, and—"

"If you say Percy, you're going to turn this conversation into a comedy."

Nic smiled, his eyes full of warmth. "He's ready to kick me out and have you move in. He's still pretty pissed off at me."

"What? He didn't get any makeup sex like I did?"

"While I did get a surprise view of his junk, I wasn't keen on sticking around to see more." He laughed, and then his expression sobered. "No strings, Sasha. Move back with us. Spend the holidays with us. And when you find work and get on your feet, I hope to God you stay."

The lump in Sasha's throat made it impossible to speak. Nic wasn't offering a job and wasn't offering something temporary. He was really asking Sasha to move in with him. Indefinitely. It was a commitment, an invitation to be part of his family. Sasha nodded, and Nic melted him with an achingly tender kiss, locking him in a warm embrace. After a few minutes of delirious cuddling, Nic withdrew to lift up on his elbows.

He nipped Sasha's chin. "If I stay here like this, we'll never leave, and that can't happen. We've got work to do today, packing up, putting notice in here, paying off your lease—"

"It's a month-to-month."

"Even better. Then I'm bringing you back home."

Home. The idea soothed him all the way through, and even his stomach pain eventually ceased nagging him. It was hard to believe everything could be so simple, that his life could get back on track in the span of one conversation, but the more time he spent with Nic, the more he believed it. The rest of the day was a blur of head-spinning bliss as they talked to the landlord and packed up his few belongings.

Backtracking was impossible with Nic. Somehow, the observant bastard always knew when Sasha was in his "peacemaker" mode. The most unfathomable part was Nic's responses when Sasha finally talked about the things that had been holding him down. He wasn't only listening. He was engaged, energized by the challenge of resolving problems and by the satisfaction of supporting Sasha like it was as necessary to him as breathing. Goddamn, he loved Nic, and the trust he never imagined he'd build again was growing steadily.

A real future stood in front of him, one where he supported Nic with the kids and with the new partnership, and, for once, one where he was supported in return. It was new and scary to lean on someone else, but Nic needed to be leaned on as much as Sasha needed to be cared for. That perfect match gave him the greatest hope of all.

Chapter Twenty-One

Nic

THE warm body pressing into Nic made him smile, and he kept his eyes closed as he savored the sensation. Sasha draped halfway across Nic, his head on Nic's pec and his right leg thrown over both of Nic's thighs. It was the first night Sasha had stayed overnight in his bed, and he'd never awoken in a better mood, proof that he'd have to keep Sasha right there every night.

A few minutes later, Sasha lifted his head. "Merry Christmas," he whispered. The press of his lips on Nic's collarbone ignited fireworks all the way through Nic. "Are you sure you're ready for today?"

"Only one way to find out. I'm used to working most of the day, followed by a long formal evening and a line of people ass-kissing my parents."

He felt Sasha's arm tighten around him. "It was good of you to give everyone today off."

"Mm. Well, you kind of changed what Christmas is for me. I'd be a dickhead to make people cook and clean up after us when they could be home with their families."

"I guess Percy'll have to change his nickname for you."

"Ha-ha, very funny." He kissed the top of Sasha's head. "I want you to wake up in my—*our*—bed every day."

Sasha tipped his head up to look Nic in the eyes. "Are you sure? The kids—"

"Love you to death and won't think anything of it." He stroked Sasha's thick blond hair back.

"Then, I want to wake up here every day too." Sasha sat up, toying with Nic's chest hair. "I ever tell you how sexy you are?"

Nic rolled and, pulling Sasha under him, growled against his ear. "I'm going to lick every in—"

Christmas music blared through the house. It had to be fairly cranked up to hear it all the way back here in Nic's bedroom.

"So much for sleeping in." Sasha laughed a full, hearty laugh, his eyes sparkling. Nic treasured that laughter more than anything in a bank account. Because he had seen and felt what it was like to lose it. *Never again.*

He smacked a kiss on the underside of Sasha's jaw and then jumped out of bed. "Let's do this Christmas thing."

It was the first time in several days they didn't shower together, but no doubt Sasha understood as well as he did that they would take too long if they weren't separate this morning. Nic still couldn't quite believe that Sasha was all his from head to foot, body and soul. What had he done to deserve all this? Whatever it was, he wasn't taking it for granted.

Wearing only worn, velvety blue jeans and a long-sleeve, charcoal Huskies T-shirt, Sasha emerged from the walk-in closet that led through to the master bath. The bright purple of the logo and lower edge of the shirt deepened Sasha's eyes to a near violet hue. He'd shaved his few days' worth of stubble in his only nod to this day being anything to dress up for. Otherwise, he was as much a lounge lizard as anyone could be. He took one look at Nic sitting cross-legged on the end of the bed working on his laptop and laughed again. The asshole.

"You can't handle this, can you? Even your pajama pants look uptight, Nic." He ruffled Nic's hair as he often enjoyed doing just to see something out of place on Nic. Something about Nic's dishevelment turned Sasha on.

"Fuck off." Nic grunted and waved him away. "Go eat breakfast with the kids. I ordered pastries yesterday and some breakfast dishes you can reheat."

He watched Sasha's eyes widen and smile falter a moment before Sasha pounced on him, gave him a hard, fast kiss, and raced out of the room. Yes, Sasha liked to point out how driven and work-obsessed Nic was. It was in his nature to take care of business, and it was equally obvious Sasha wasn't quite used to being Nic's business to take care of. It was like every nice thing he did for Sasha was some huge, wondrous surprise. How badly had Drew and the others before used Sasha to drill that response in?

He clenched his jaw, his determination set. He was going to show every day, especially today, that he could be the man Sasha and the kids deserved and needed. A shower and shave later, Nic threw on the outfit he'd purchased especially for this morning and grabbed a huge red velvet bag full of wrapped gifts.

Stopping by the den, he set his bag near the tree. They'd given it a makeover a few days earlier, the lights all different colors and the ornaments all mismatched, and it was the most beautiful tree he'd ever seen. He and Sasha had decided to keep the tree itself and only strip the plain white décor because, though the noble fir lacked character, it was a nice, tall, bushy one.

"Hey, Uncle Nic, aren't you going to—" Ben lurched to a stop, Lucy running directly into his back at the suddenness of it. Sasha and Percy followed behind, both with matching expressions of disbelief.

"What? You've never seen Santa before or something?" He looked down at his red and white costume with the wide black belt hanging low on his hips. Of course, it was a way to avoid facing the ridicule he logically knew wouldn't come but had been conditioned to expect, his gut reacting to the expectation. His parents would have ripped him apart for dressing up like Santa or even acknowledging the concept of a Santa Claus.

Strong arms wound around his waist before he could look back up. "Daaaamn, Santa. You work out or something?" Sasha's low rumble against his throat made him smile, and then more arms wrapped around him along with a chorus of Merry Christmases.

Percy hooked an arm over Nic's neck. He couldn't remember the last time he'd seen Percy smile so widely. "You do know Santa has a jelly belly, right?"

"Suck it, Percy. I need my ridiculousness in small doses. Besides, I'm paleo Santa, and at least I have the beard. Who knew it would be so itchy?" He tugged it down to rest around his collarbone.

Lucy gasped. "Uncle Nic? You're Santa?"

He grabbed her and rubbed that itchy beard on her face, laughing with her. When he settled her under his arm, she was wearing the beard, and Ben was snapping away with Sasha's camera. His stomach lurched before he took a second to self-soothe, reminding himself this wasn't his parents' day-long Christmas event where everything had to be posed like a mannequin display and any play was rewarded with harsh censure. Guess he was still adjusting as much as Sasha.

"I don't know how Christmas is supposed to go, but waiting for the presents will kill me, so if it's the same to you, I'd like to do it now."

"You had me at presents," Percy said.

They settled on the sofas, and Sasha handed Nic a lemon-blueberry scone, his favorite, and a fresh coffee. He brushed his fingers over Sasha's as he accepted the plate, then took a bite and set it down before pulling two envelopes from the wide pockets on his Santa suit. He handed one each to Lucy and Ben.

They looked at each other but didn't say anything. Lucy nodded to Ben to go first. He opened it, and Nic's stomach took a dive. What if he'd picked wrong? Maybe the gift was too much and Ben would think he was trying to buy his way in.

The kid rubbed a hand over his head as he stared at the card inside. "Is this what I think? Is it real?"

"It's real. I wish I would have done it sooner."

At the badgering of the others, Ben showed them the pictures inside. "It's a dance studio. Added on right here in the house."

"It's not all that big, but it'll have the sprung floors and mirrors and everything."

With a choked cry, Ben dodged the coffee table and tackle-hugged Nic. "I didn't think you knew."

"Kid," Nic said with a sigh when Ben returned to his seat, "I know so much more than you think. I'm sorry I haven't been around as much as I should have, but I've always loved you."

Lucy's fingers danced around the corners of her envelope, the only thing betraying her nerves, but her expression was calm. Sasha had been right. She'd do well in a boardroom full of investors. Or, knowing Lucy, a table full of pro poker players.

She tugged the lip open and stared at her card for a few seconds, her eyebrows lowering. "What is this? There's no way this is happening."

"Yeah, it is. She's here. I mean, not here but on Vashon. We need to build a barn first to keep her here, but she's boarded nearby for now."

"Uncle Nic." Tears filled her eyes when she looked up at him. She held up the pictures of a glossy black mare. "You remembered."

"Of course, Lucy." He shrugged helplessly, never having been one to know how to deal with tears, especially when it came to the children. What would Sasha do? With that in mind, he stepped over the table and sat next to her, pulling her against him. "It's all you ever asked for every time I saw you from the time you were two years old. Then one day you stopped and never again asked for anything you truly wanted."

She drew back, her jade eyes meeting his. There was no need to explain what day that was. It was too painful for either of them to mention.

He cleared his throat. "So, she's a Morgan, and I have to mention she was a package deal. Her companion's a Welsh cross pony she couldn't live without. We'll do something soon about a barn and pasture for them."

"I didn't know you could have horses around here," Sasha said.

Percy answered, which made sense since he'd had Percy look into the codes and regulations to make sure it was feasible. "This whole island is horse-friendly. You can ride all over here, and there are a few parks with riding trails."

"What'd you get for Percy, Uncle Nic?" Ben asked.

He laughed as he returned to his spot next to Sasha. "Percy knows already, and I'm not telling unless he wants to share."

It took a few minutes of peer pressure, but Percy finally caved in. "Have I mentioned how much you all suck? I didn't want anyone to know how petty I am," he admitted. "Okay, so I ended a bad—to put it lightly— relationship a little over a year ago. The bastard kept my cat. I got my Maine Coon kitten before my ex and I lived together, but he won the court case."

"He took you to court over it? Who the fuck does that?" Sasha asked.

"I did say he was a bastard, didn't I?" He shook his head. "Nic finally got dirt on the guy and forced him to sign Pinky back over. I get him back right after the New Year starts."

"A giant Maine Coon named Pinky?" Lucy laughed as she asked.

"It's a nickname. He had a thing for Pinky and the Brain, followed Pinky all over the screen." He sent Nic a look of gratitude and a grin. "Nothing like a little extortion on my behalf to make my Christmas."

Nic turned to Sasha and took his hand. "I had trouble with yours. I wanted to shower you with new, expensive things. I wanted to treat you to things you'd never imagined having before, things that would impress you. No matter what I thought of, though, it wasn't enough. In the end, they were all just... things. I wanted this to mean something to you. So I hope you don't mind that your gift isn't new, and it isn't expensive. Well, it isn't to me."

Freeing his hands, he pulled a small remote from his other wide pocket and worked the controls. A loud whirr preceded the arrival of a remote control truck.

"Holy shit," Sasha mumbled. "It's my truck. How'd you even find an RC that close to mine?" A laugh burst from him. "The elf? The elf on the shelf stole my truck?"

Nic guided the miniature Silverado with the elf in the tiny truck bed right to Sasha's feet. It had taken him a couple practice sessions to make sure he could successfully pull off the delivery without running the toy straight into a wall. Percy, bless the man, had helped his hopeless ass.

He knew the moment Sasha saw his gift, the sharp gasp giving him away.

"Nic." Sasha didn't say anything more as he lifted the familiar key fob from the elf's arms and stared at it a long while. Then, he leaned over until his face was buried against Nic's throat, and Nic cradled him there, cupping the back of Sasha's head and ignoring the dampness from Sasha's face. Giving him a moment to feel overwhelmed and then contain it. Sasha hated crying as much as Nic did, especially in front of witnesses. Such emotions had been something they'd both been raised to suppress but somehow had both found safe to express with each other.

"Well," Sasha said as he leaned back. "That's enough of that. Thank you, Nic. This was perfect. So perfect."

Percy stood and grabbed a large gift to hand to Nic. "We all got together and discussed the dilemma of what to gift someone who has the money to buy anything he wants."

Lifting a brow, Nic shrugged. "A jet? I don't have that yet."

"Yeah, we'll spend your money to buy your present." Lucy rolled her eyes. "Shut up, Uncle Nic, and open your present. This one's from me and Ben."

Nic tore into the wrapping, and cathartic didn't do that action justice. He'd never been allowed this, always expected to carefully remove the tape and fold the paper or the box like a "civilized" person. Shredding and ripping gave him enough satisfaction that a gift wasn't even necessary.

But he changed his mind once he saw the gift and Ben explained. "We decided we didn't want to give a billionaire things. Instead, we want to give you time. That's the best gaming system we could find with a ton of memory. Sasha said it's perfect, and they have any kind of game you'd want. Sasha said you didn't get to play enough games when you were little, so we're going to teach you."

The air caught in his lungs as he smoothed his hand over the box. Teach him? They'd already begun. All this time, he'd been an outsider to them only to learn that his belief in being the outsider was what held him there.

"You have no idea what this means to me. Thank you for this. I can't wait to get it set up. You guys up for playing later today?"

"Hell yes!"

"Ben, language," Percy corrected automatically. Then, without pausing, he continued. "Nic, Sasha and I worked on something together, the same concept of time instead of things. My contribution is to take care

of the kids, the house, and all your business for the next
few weeks. You're welcome. Sasha?"

With a stunning grin, Sasha took Nic's hands in
his. "Nic—fuck, this is even better now that I have my
truck back." He shook his head. "Nic, will you road trip
with me? I want to take you all up and down the coast,
stopping at every little tourist trap we feel like, eating
the most delicious clam chowder and fish and chips the
world's ever known, tearing up the sand dunes, catching
our dinner on the Pacific before camping under the
stars, and any other crazy, fun, frivolous, nerdy thing
we can think of doing."

His answer for Sasha was a full-body embrace.

"I can't wait for that either," Nic whispered. And
then he kissed Sasha in front of the kids. Obviously,
they'd never been a secret, but they'd both been fairly
secretive in how demonstrative they'd been in public.
He couldn't have asked for better children to raise,
though. They both laughed and whooped, clapping and
then whistling.

Percy stood up again. "Kids, let's get this system
set up in the theater. Shit, the graphics are gonna be
incredible."

After another chorus of Merry Christmases and
thank-yous, Lucy and Ben followed Percy out with the
console and box of games, leaving Nic gazing deeply into
Sasha's eyes. He could drown in that ocean, the emotions
rising like a tide as they always did with Sasha.

Then Sasha drew back and sighed, his tongue
darting out to moisten his lips and his hands clamped
tightly. Something was bothering him. Nic had learned
the signs rather quickly. Sasha continued to have
difficulty opening up about his troubles and probably
would for some time, but that would never stop Nic
from trying to help him through it and earn his complete

trust. Funny how it was so easy for Sasha when it was about other people but caring for himself seemed to stick in his throat.

Nic had also learned not to push but to pull gently when Sasha was having the hardest time. He leaned forward and rubbed Sasha's thigh, the soft denim enticing over the hard muscle beneath.

Sasha laughed suddenly. "You're getting turned on."

"How could I not? We're alone, and that shirt shows every detail of your chest." Nic flicked one of Sasha's nipples.

"Fuck, you're making it hard to get this out."

"Am I? I think you're making it hard." Nic guided Sasha's hand over to Nic's groin. He chuckled, pulling his hand away.

A puff of breath, and then Sasha started talking. "I want this trip to be amazing." Nic nodded wordlessly, knowing Sasha would say more if Nic didn't speak. "I want to go everywhere and not worry about running out of... well, running out of money."

Ah, and there was the problem. It probably wasn't fair there was such a wide disparity in wealth between him and Sasha, but life was like that. Nic didn't give two shits, but it mattered to Sasha—understandably. Nic couldn't imagine how it would feel if the tables were reversed, but Sasha was wealthier than Nic in so many other ways. He just had to get Sasha to see it, and he was willing to spend a lifetime doing that.

"I do owe you Thanksgiving holiday pay and your hiring bonus and your severance package from when I fired you."

The corners of Sasha's lips curled slightly. He obviously knew what Nic was doing, providing him money without the appearance of a handout. The tension in his shoulders melted away, along with the worry Nic had seen in his expression.

"I love you, Nic. I don't think I've ever had a better Christmas than being here with you and Percy and the kids."

Nic pulled Sasha under his arm and leaned back into the sofa. "Love you too, so much. I've never even had a real Christmas."

And he hadn't, not really. Now he understood what he'd never known before, what Christmas spirit was. He let it wash over him as they nestled on the couch for a while before finally getting up to shove some of the Christmas meal into the ovens, a prime rib and a smoked ham. Sasha was a fantastic home cook and taught Nic a lot as they prepped a few dishes. The rest of the herd wandered in a little later to help.

The remainder of the day they spent playing on the console, eventually splitting into competitive teams. They raided their stockings and ate too much candy right before Christmas dinner. The kids begged for champagne and got it, finding it as disgusting as Nic had hoped they would. They ended the evening with a Christmas movie in the theater, and with his fingers entwined in Sasha's, Nic couldn't stop smiling at the memory of tormenting him during their last movie night.

Funny that nearly two months earlier, he'd believed he was nothing without Leighton Price. A fucking company. How wrong he'd been to think work could come close to fulfilling him the way Sasha did. This man was his bridge, his guide, and his light. Tonight, he would show Sasha how much he loved everything about him. He'd show him the slow burn of making love last all night. Then maybe he could keep his manny forever and make that love last all their lives.

Coming in January 2019

REAMSPUN DESIRES

Dreamspun Desires #73
The Athlete and the Aristocrat by Louisa Masters
Sometimes love takes balls.

Newly retired championship footballer Simon Wood is taking on his next challenge. His plan for a charity to provide funding for underprivileged children to pursue football as a career has passed its first hurdle: he has backers and an executive consultant. Now it's time to get the ball rolling.

Lucien Morel, heir to the multibillion-euro Morel Corporation, is shocked—and thrilled—to learn his father has volunteered him as consultant to a fledgling football charity. Better yet, the brains behind it all is heartthrob Simon Wood, his teenage idol and crush.

Although Simon and Lucien get off on the wrong foot, it's not long before they're getting along like a house on fire—sparks included. But with the charity under public scrutiny, can their romance thrive?

Dreamspun Desires #74
Whiskey and Moonshine by Elizabeth Noble
Drunk on love.

Like a well-aged whiskey, master distiller and old-money entrepreneur Malone Kensington is elegant and refined. Unfortunately he's also a perfectionist who is more dedicated to the success of his generations-old company than his own love life.

That company needs a public spokesman.

What Colton Hale lacks in sophistication, he more than makes up for with the charisma that's allowed him to survive on the street from a young age and charm his way into the lucrative—if overwhelming—public position at the Kensington Distillery. When Mal takes Colt under his wing, hoping to polish off his rough edges, opposites attract and a passionate romance blossoms despite the differences in age and background. But can it survive a Kensington Board of Directors who believe Colt is nothing but a gold digger and a kidnapper determined to profit from the love of Mal's life—dead or alive?

Love Always Finds a Way